WITCH ON TRIAL

A BLAIR WILKES MYSTERY

ELLE ADAMS

O f all the things I'd expected to be doing on a first date, climbing under a waterfall in search of pixie dust definitely wasn't one of them.

I'd had my fair share of abnormal experiences ever since I'd moved to the paranormal town of Fairy Falls a few months ago, but my quest for the elf king might be the weirdest yet. And the last week had involved a tussle with my best friend on the back of a broomstick and finding the witch who owned the town napping in a coffin, among other things. Nathan and I looked up at the curtain of water splashing into the deep pool below. The elf king had asked me to bring him a rare plant which supposedly grew under the Fairy Falls, but I couldn't see anything except rocks and water sprinkled with a hint of glitter.

"I'm sure it's here somewhere." I crouched down beside the curtain of water, resisting the impulse to dunk my head underneath it as I'd done once before. Nathan took my arm to stop me from falling in, probably a wise move. I hardly believed he'd actually come with me after my immense stupidity of late had almost wrecked our potential relationship before it even got off the ground. Admittedly, he'd also helped arrest my dad in his days as a paranormal hunter working as a prison security guard. And I'd deceived him about being a fairy for the first few weeks we'd known one another, thinking that he'd see me as a freak. I'd turned out to be wrong. Not only was he willing to forgive me, and I him, he'd come with me on my ridiculous quest to find a long-extinct plant that was rumoured to grow somewhere… hang on a moment.

I leaned forward and squinted up at the jagged rock face behind the falls. "I think there's something growing up there."

The plant called pixie dust might be listed as extinct, but I'd looked it up in two different textbooks and I had the image memorised. A faint shimmer on the leaves growing from the rock face confirmed my suspicions. Problem: it was way out of reach.

Nathan tilted his head back to look up at the falls. "Can those boots of yours reach it?"

"I think so," I said, looking down at my Seven Millimetre Boots. They had their limitations, but because they could travel in any direction, I could use them to fly as well as walking quicker than usual. I stood on tip-toe, feeling the spray of water from the falls. "But flying is easier."

"Are you sure?" he asked. "I can wait here, but if you go under the falls, I won't be able to catch you."

"I won't fall in if I de-glamour." I snapped the fingers of my right hand and wings unfurled behind my shoulders. In fairy mode, my skin was glittery and my ears pointed, but aside from that, I supposedly looked the same as before. Being half fairy and half witch had been a bumpy ride so far, but what mattered was that Nathan didn't mind. That was enough for me.

"Be careful." He briefly touched my arm, making my heart jump in my chest, and then I beat my wings and left the bank.

The curtain of water crashed down inches away from me as I flew closer to the plant growing at the back. It did match the illustration. The elf king hadn't tried to trick me after all. Taking a quest from an elf was generally unwise, but in exchange for the pixie dust, the elf king had promised to tell me why my father had come to the forest a few years ago. The father I'd never met. While my foster parents loved me unconditionally, the fact that my magical birth family were still out there and hadn't got in touch had been bothering me ever since I'd moved here. If I got hold of the glitter-tinted plant growing behind the falls, I'd get at least one answer about my past.

I beat my fairy wings and hovered awkwardly in front of the falls, getting drenched in the process. Taking a breath, I flew to the side of the falls, reaching higher to get into a position to pull the leaves out of the rock. Grabbing them firmly in hand, I pulled hard. The leaves didn't move. I pulled again, putting all the strength I had into it, but the leaves clung fast.

"I can help." Nathan leaned off the bank, reaching out with both hands. "I'll hold onto you, while you pull."

I let go of the leaves and flew back so he could reach me. Then I extended my arm and gripped the leaves again. "Okay, sure."

He grabbed my waist and pulled. The leaves came free,

and I fell backwards into him, pulling both of us off the bank and into the water.

A roaring torrent crashed over my head, and I kicked to the surface, spitting out a mouthful of water. Nathan emerged a moment later.

"Ah." I pushed my sodden hair from my face, treading water. "Sorry about that."

"Did you get them?" he asked, grabbing the side of the bank with one hand.

"Yes." I spotted the leaves floating a few feet away and plucked them out of the water.

Nathan pulled himself out, his hair plastered to his face.

"Sorry." I swam to the bank, clutching the leaves in one hand. "I can't keep my balance even with wings."

He laughed and reached out a hand to help me out of the water. I took it, awkwardly climbed up the bank and would have fallen onto my face if he hadn't caught my arm and kissed me.

Oh. Now that was worth waiting for.

He pushed my soaking hair out of my eyes. "Should I not have done that?"

"No, I've been waiting for a while." I grinned stupidly for a minute. My clothes were soaked. So were my wings, though I'd forgotten I was in fairy mode at all. Nathan moved back to give me some space to squeeze the water from my hair. His soaking wet clothes clung to him in a way that made me almost forget the leaves I'd dropped on the bank. I picked them up, shedding glitter. Oh no. I looked back at Nathan, who was similarly decorated. The glitter had even ended up in his hair.

"I know a drying spell." I reached for my wand, which

had luckily stayed in my pocket. With one wave, my clothes were dry. A moment later, so were Nathan's.

"Nice job." He looked down at his newly dried clothes. "I haven't seen that one before."

"Alissa taught it to me. It's supposed to be a hair-drying spell, but it works for anything." I put my wand away. "You don't mind walking back to town like that? We shouldn't run into any hunters at least, but you should know you have pink glitter in your hair."

He tilted his head. "I think I'll survive it. You got what you needed, right?"

"Yeah. I'll hand it over to the elf king first thing tomorrow."

"You're back at work tomorrow?"

I nodded. "Assuming Veronica comes back to town in time. I know they found her, but I'm not sure she took a broomstick like Alissa."

My boss had been hit with a spell which caused her to impulsively run off in search of her shifter ex-husband, the same spell that had turned my best friend into a broomstick-riding daredevil. The spell was off now, and the person who'd accidentally caused it—Rebecca, the younger sister of my ex-co-worker Blythe—would be starting magical training as soon as possible to ensure it didn't happen again. Meanwhile, their manipulative mother was in jail for trying to force her daughter to use her powers to help her take over the town council and dismantle the covens. Thanks to the chaos they'd caused, it'd taken me until the day before the elf king's deadline to track down the pixie dust. But now all I had it, I'd finally be able to find out some of my birth family's history.

I was one step closer to the truth.

————

The following morning, I woke bright and early to a claw poking my leg.

"Miaow," said Sky, the little cat I'd adopted. Or who'd adopted me, depending on who you asked. Black with one white front paw, he had one blue eye and one grey, and it'd taken far too long to figure out he was a fairy cat and not a witch's familiar.

Another jab to my knee. "Miaow."

"What?" I looked up blearily. There was an elf outside my window, his little pointed face pressed against the glass.

I jumped out of bed. "He might have given me chance to bring it in person. It's dawn." Admittedly, I was cutting it close to the elf king's deadline, but I'd spent the week saving the town. Grabbing a dressing gown and slippers, I picked up the leaves as well as my keys before running out into the garden.

Between rows of flowering plants stood the elf who'd taken me into the elven kingdom last time. He was about four feet tall and wore bark-coloured clothes. His pointed ears were not unlike my own when I was in fairy mode, but I was firmly in sleepy human mode at the moment.

"Blair Wilkes," he said. "Today is your deadline to bring what the elf king desires."

"I was going to bring it later, but I have what he wanted." I held out the clump of leaves.

The elf snatched the pixie dust from my hand. "I will take it to him," he said. "And if he wishes to speak to you, he will."

"But we had a deal," I protested. "He was supposed to tell me what happened when he saw my dad—"

"Come with me to the king when he asks, not before." With a swift bow, he was gone, disappearing into the bushes.

"Excuse me?" I stared after him. "I should have known he'd go back on his word." Elves were known for being tricky, but I'd risked life and limb to get those leaves. Okay, I'd got close to Nathan in the process, but come on.

A flash of glitter made my head snap up. A pixie had appeared, fluttering around my head. "Too late. He's gone."

The pixie dropped a piece of paper on my head. I jumped, causing the paper to fall to the ground, and dove to retrieve the note.

It was from my dad, though he never signed his correspondence.

I'm glad to hear you're safe. It's too risky to say much on paper in case this letter falls into the wrong hands, but I want you to know I never meant to abandon you in the normal world. Your mother and I had very good reason for leaving you behind, and your own safety was paramount. I'd like to keep in touch and see you the next time I'm able to.

I blinked tears from my eyes. My safety. I'd spent years coming up with reasonable explanations as to why my birth parents hadn't kept in touch with me, ranging from them being superheroes to them having moved abroad and forgotten about me. But in my hand was definitive proof that my dad had wanted to see me and had been prevented from doing so by forces beyond his control.

But how he wound up in jail? I understood why he'd

thought it was too risky to put that information in a letter, but I wished I knew more.

I looked up at the pixie. "Can you please ask the elf king to invite me to come and see him today? We had an arrangement and he promised me information." He might know nothing at all, and besides, the elves didn't seem to like the pixie much. No, it was more likely that I'd have to wait until whenever the king felt it was convenient to speak to me. Which might be never.

When the pixie vanished, I left the garden and returned to the house. It was the nicest place I'd ever lived in, a pretty impressive manor-sized establishment that belonged to Madame Grey, the witch who owned the whole town. Alissa and I rented one ground-floor flat, but it was more than enough for two people and two demanding cats.

Alissa was in the kitchen making coffee when I came in. "I thought you were going to elf land," she said.

"Nope. The elf took the leaves and ran off, and apparently the king's going to call me back... whenever. Not sure they have a phone signal deep in the woods."

"That seems unfair. You did complete his quest. At least you got—wait, what's that note?" She indicated the paper clutched in my hand.

"A letter. From my dad." I took a seat on the sofa, where Sky promptly joined me, much to the annoyance of Roald, Alissa's cat. I didn't know if Sky was more demanding because he was a fairy cat or if it was just his personality, but whenever he was in the room, Roald would get a swipe if he went too close to me. "He didn't say much. Just that he apparently had good reason not to get in touch with me, but he can't tell me what it is."

"I don't blame him for wanting to be cautious about sharing information in a letter," said Alissa. "Especially if it might fall into someone else's hands. I mean, I'm guessing the people at the jail don't know he's passing on messages to you via the pixie."

"Not just me," I said. "He was in touch with Lord Goddard too—he must have been, there's no other way for him to have known Peter the wizard was after me. I think he and the pixie must be friends, but it's not like we can speak the same language."

Peter the crazy wizard was locked up where he belonged, but he was a recent threat. My parents had left me in the normal world, with no clue I was paranormal, when I was mere days old. Now I knew my dad was locked in the region's most secure paranormal prison, it made a little more sense that he'd given me up for adoption. And I had nothing to complain about as far as my foster family were concerned. They were loving, caring… and entirely normal.

"Maybe you can figure out how to talk to the pixie," Alissa said, setting two mugs down on the table. Specially enhanced mood-boosting witch tea, judging by the fruity smell. "Don't forget you have the book."

"Oh, yeah." I moved to the bookshelf and retrieved the thick volume titled, *The General Guide to Fairies and Other Species*, skipping to the section on 'pixies'.

Apparently, pixie dialect wasn't comprehensible to anyone except their own species. Fairies also had their own language, though like Elvish, it was spoken only in their small communities and since they'd mingled with humans more than elves had, it was on its way to extinction.

I put the book down and took a sip of warm, berry-flavoured tea. "You know, fairies are probably much more common in other paranormal communities. I just happened to wind up in one where I'm the novelty."

I'd begun to grow used to the stares, though admittedly I'd had much more important things on my mind in the last week. But the town was steeped in fairy history that seemed to be lost from records. Even the Fairy Falls themselves. Legend told that fairies had once lived there, but not a single one had surfaced in so long that even the town's oldest resident, a seven-hundred-year-old vampire, had no recollection.

I picked up a pen and tore a piece of paper loose from my work notepad. "Hmm... what do I ask my dad this time? If he can't share anything that might fall into the wrong hands, then that shuts down a lot of conversation topics. I obviously can't ask why he gave me up for adoption, or why he was jailed."

"Ask if any of your other family members are still alive," Alissa suggested. "Just a yes or no would do, he wouldn't have to go into details."

"Yeah, but that wouldn't give me much to go by." I slumped back, chewing on my pen. "How do you even begin to connect with a family member you've never actually met? I don't know him. And you know, he *is* in jail for some crime he won't tell me about."

"He helped you find out Peter the wizard's plan," Alissa reminded me. "I'd say he cares for you and he's looking out for you."

"Yeah." That should be enough. And yet a sliver of doubt remained, fed by the words Blythe's mother had said in front of the entire witch council.

Your parents were common thieves.

I didn't believe her—didn't *want* to believe her—but she'd believed she told the truth. And my lie-sensing power hadn't picked up on any deception.

I still wasn't sure whether my lie-sensing power was a witch one or a fairy one. The stories said fairies couldn't lie, which suggested that power belonged to my fairy side, but to make things confusing, the witch side of my family boasted some pretty strong mind powers. My mother, Tanith Wildflower, had been a powerful witch. Unlike my dad, she'd grown up in Fairy Falls, though she'd left a couple of years before I was born, and nobody had seen either of them since.

Until now. The piece of paper in my hand was a fragile connection to my history. I was an anomaly, but I'd finally begun to accept I wasn't just a freak.

———

I arrived at work in a decent mood despite my lingering annoyance at the elf king for not even acknowledging that I'd held up my end of the bargain. I'd sent the pixie off with the reply to my dad's note, so now it was time to fix the mess the boss's disappearance had caused over the last week. Dritch & Co was a paranormal recruitment agency, so we dealt with finding suitable employees for our vampire, witch and wizard clients. Three of the staff had been hit by Blythe's sister's personality-altering spell— unluckily, at the precise moment when we'd been told to find new people to train to be part of the town's security force. These days, security was more important than ever.

The blond receptionist gave me a strained smile when

I walked in.

"Hey, Callie," I said. "Glad to see you're back."

"I'm so sorry, Blair!" she said. "I can't believe I shifted when the paranormal hunters were on the phone. I hope that won't make trouble for you."

"We drove them out of town," I said. "They won't come back without Madame Grey's say-so. Besides, you weren't to know you were under a spell."

"I should have," she said. "It's not like it's the first time it's happened. My dad isn't happy."

He never is. Chief Donovan was wildly overprotective of his daughter and his werewolf pack as a whole, and the shifters were the most likely to kick up a fuss if the paranormal hunters came within sniffing distance of the town. Luckily for all of us, the three hunters who Blythe's mother had picked to help her out weren't the brightest bulbs and had disappeared the instant Nathan got the police involved. But thanks to someone putting them on our call list—not to mention Callie's shifting and growling at them down the phone—our town was officially on the hunters' radar.

I went into the main office through the wooden door on the left of the reception. Lizzie, the tall, dark-skinned computer expert of the office was fiddling with the printer, while Bethan, the boss's daughter, was in the middle of moving half a ton of papers onto my desk. Spotting me, she gave me an apologetic look and began shifting them back to her own. Her thick dark hair swept over her shoulder, and the shadows under her eyes stood out against her pale skin. She'd probably been up all night looking for Veronica.

"Your mum's not back yet?" I asked. There was no sign

of Lena, the fourth member of our team, but she'd found our work environment chaotic and alarming even before the spell had hit her, which was a fair assessment. From wrangling unicorn handlers to dealing with cantankerous wand-makers, there was never a dull moment at the appropriately-named Eldritch & Co.

"She'll be here in a bit," said Bethan. "She got back in the early hours of the morning, so she's had to check in at home first. She'd flown halfway to Scotland when they caught up to her."

"So she did take a broomstick? What about Lena?"

"I don't know if she'll want to come back, to be honest," said Bethan. "We did track her down, but I think she's written the town off as a hazard."

"So we're back to just three of us again." Lizzie took a seat at her desk. "I hope the boss is at the top of her game, because this mess isn't going to sort itself out."

"Veronica's back to normal, for what it's worth," Bethan responded, shuffling papers. "Oh, she's here."

From the lobby came a familiar voice. Then the office door opened and Veronica Eldritch strode in. The boss was tall and lean like her daughter, but with white hair instead of black. Her arms were full of papers and her dark skirt and white shirt were more wrinkled than usual, but it was a huge relief to see her.

"Oh, good, you're all here," she said. "I have to apologise for leaving you in the lurch. Were you able to complete this paperwork?"

There was an awkward silence.

"Not exactly," said Bethan. "Half the phone numbers didn't work. I tried to call a witch in Bolton and got a troll in Reykjavik instead."

"And the number for the esteemed Yorkshire Wizard ended up being the number for a satyr-owned dry-cleaning company in Essex," Lizzie put in.

Veronica's brows rose as we explained the chaotic week we'd had. Not only had she disappeared, none of her instructions had made any sense and nearly all the client details were wrong. Normally, Veronica was efficient enough to be mildly terrifying, with a literal paranormal ability to keep track of countless details at once. The rest of us had been left floundering in her absence.

Veronica picked up the topmost paper on the stack from Bethan's desk. "Oh, this is an easy fix. We'll be back to normal by Monday."

I suspected we'd be working overtime for a while, but it was better than having no boss at all.

"The more up to date files are in my office," Veronica said. "I'll be back in a second."

She darted out of the office, and a current of air blew in, prompting me and Bethan to move to stop the papers from toppling off the desk.

There was the sound of a door opening, a soft gasp, then silence.

Bethan steadied the papers and got to her feet. "Er, are you okay, Mum?"

No response. Shooting me a look of alarm, Bethan ran to the half-open door and out into the reception area. When she gasped, too, I ran to join her.

Veronica stood in front of her partially open office door. A man lay across her path, not moving, like he'd just fallen out of the office. "Well," said Veronica. "That wasn't there when I left."

No kidding. The man was dead.

2

Callie called the police from reception. Veronica tried to deposit the papers on her desk until Bethan pointed out that the cause of the man's death might be inside her office, at which point she dumped them on the floor of the lobby and started casting decontamination spells around the whole place.

Naturally, that's when Steve the Gargoyle walked in.

The chief of police was a huge hulking man even when he had his wings hidden beneath his baggy blue uniform. My paranormal sensing ability showed me images of stone cliff faces when he narrowed his eyes at me. "Why is it always you, Blair? What have you done now?"

"Don't look at me," I said. "None of us have been here since the boss vanished two days ago. We didn't kill the guy, whoever he is."

"Clearly, you're here *now*," he said. "Who was the last person to go into that room?"

"Uh," said Bethan. "We all did. I mean, Blair, Lizzie and I went in there on Wednesday to check if my mother left any clues behind. There definitely weren't any dead bodies in there. He just fell out when Mum opened the door, so he must have been there this morning. Or yesterday."

"This room's supposed to be protected against trespassers," said Veronica. "If he got in, he must have broken the protective wards."

"Who even is he?" I asked. "A wizard?"

He was a plain man, maybe forty-five or so, with greying hair and a lime green jacket and pressed trousers. A teacher, I'd guess at a glance, but my paranormal sensing power didn't seem to work on the dead. It did on the *un*dead, but maybe vampires were different.

"Yes, he's a wizard," said Veronica. "His name is Dr Appleton. An old business partner of mine. I suppose the wards on the room came down in my absence and he broke in." She spoke matter-of-factly. For someone who dealt with as many paranormal clients as she did, maybe he wasn't the first dead body she'd seen. But Steve didn't look impressed.

"You seem to have given this a great deal of thought," he said, as the front door opened and several other gargoyles entered. "Have you ever attacked a trespasser before?"

"Are you accusing me of killing this man?" asked Veronica. "You might want to determine the cause of death first."

"Don't tell me how to do my job," Steve said irritably.

He'd had pretty much the same response whenever I'd tried to help the police, but I still felt indignation on my boss's part. And worry. She hadn't even been here, so she couldn't have killed the guy, but let's just say Steve was a little trigger-happy.

"You're going to stay put, all of you. Especially you, Blair." Steve advanced on Veronica. "You'll be questioned first. You four, get in there."

Two gargoyles shepherded Bethan, Lizzie, Callie and me back into our office. Apparently, Steve intended to run the interrogations in the lobby of all places. The office felt more cramped than usual with the gargoyles standing amid the stacks of papers which would probably never get dealt with at this rate.

The printer made a spluttering noise. One of the gargoyles turned on it with narrowed eyes. "What was that?"

"The printer," said Lizzie, moving in that direction. "We haven't been here in a couple of days, and it doesn't like being left alone."

"Doesn't like?" echoed the gargoyle. "Is it alive?"

The printer spat a wad of paper at him. The gargoyle snarled in anger, hurling the paper to the floor. "How dare you attack me!"

"I didn't touch it," Lizzie protested. "It hasn't been looked at for two days. Maybe it's jammed. I can check."

"Don't leave this room," said the gargoyle. He pointedly moved right behind her as she opened the printer's insides. A jet of ink shot out, hitting him in the face. I stifled a laugh as he swore and backed away from the printer, his face drenched in black and blue ink.

"Blair, can you help?" asked Lizzie.

"I'm not going into that thing," I said. "You know it doesn't like me."

The gargoyle looked at me like I had two heads. Even

in the paranormal world, a semi-sentient printer was an oddity, but Lizzie's gift for dealing with magical technology held no equal. Didn't mean I wanted to be splattered with ink, though. The gargoyle grabbed a wad of paper and tried to clean his face, but succeeded only in smearing the ink all the way down to his neck.

Bethan and I ducked for cover behind the desk as more ink flew out of the printer, splattering the office wall in neon stripes.

"Sorry!" Lizzie yelped. "I don't know what the problem is—maybe it's scared of gargoyles."

This is going well.

Ten minutes of dodging ink projectiles later, Veronica returned to the office from her interview with Steve.

"What is going on in here?" She indicated the ink-splattered gargoyle, whose face now bore an interesting spotted marble effect.

"They're making trouble, as usual," growled Ink Face.

"The printer got jammed when I wasn't here," Lizzie explained, ink staining her own arms from where she'd buried them in the printer. "I was trying to fix it."

"Yes, do that," Veronica said, turning to Ink Face. "As for you two, kindly don't make a mess of my office."

"You're in no position to be ordering anyone around," Steve said from behind her. "You, Bethan Eldritch, will come in for questioning next. You're Veronica's daughter, so maybe you caught the victim breaking into her office and retaliated."

"I haven't opened her office since she disappeared," Bethan said, looking outraged. "But—now you mention it, Veronica, the protection spells weren't up on Wednesday. I didn't think to reset them."

"This isn't your fault, Bethan," Veronica said, abruptly switching to a more serious manner. "My daughter is *not* the killer. Dr Appleton died when his head hit the cabinet. Maybe he tripped and fell."

"That's what a murderer would say," Steve said. "Miss Eldritch, come with me."

Bethan obeyed, while the rest of us remained in the office, Veronica included.

"Uh," I said. "Do you know why that man was in your office? None of the rest of us knew the guy."

"Clearly he was breaking in," said Veronica. "He wasn't supposed to be here when I was absent."

Truth, said my lie-sensing power. Or she believed it to be true, anyway.

"But why break in?" I asked. "To steal something from your office?"

"I keep all the information on past clients in my office," she said, eyeing the stack of paperwork. "It's an easy shortcut if he wanted to find something out. Name, job history, even paranormal type."

True. Though there were limitations. I'd vetted clients myself using my paranormal sensing power, and found a werewolf pretending to be a wizard, among other things. But if the dead man was just here to get information, who'd followed and killed him?

"He can't have been a good wizard," said Lizzie. "There's not much you can't find out about someone with a divining spell. Was he part of a coven?"

"Not to my knowledge," said Veronica. "His death, however, has nothing to do with me."

"It clearly wasn't an accident," snarled Ink Face.

"I never said it was," said Veronica. "After all, that's what Steve thinks."

Steve couldn't add two and two with a calculator. "Maybe he was here to ask for your help. And… uh, someone was chasing him and caught up before you came back?"

"You're not the one running the interrogation, Blair Wilkes," growled Ink Face.

"No, but none of us is the killer," I said firmly. "We haven't been here in two days."

The printer contributed by spitting another jet of ink across the office. Once again, I dove for cover under the desk.

Ten very long minutes later, Steve returned. "Blair Wilkes, it's your turn for questioning."

I'd expected as much. While Bethan joined her mother in the office, I obligingly went into the reception area for questioning. Steve had commandeered Callie's desk and draped his huge gargoyle form behind it, wings out and all. His skin was marble grey in full gargoyle mode, while his personality was even more rigid than usual. The dead man still lay in the doorway of Veronica's office, presumably until Steve gave the go-ahead to move him. Being interrogated in front of the half-open eyes of a dead person was distracting to say the least.

"I don't know who he is," I said, looking at the gargoyle rather than the dead man. "Nor how he got into the boss's office. How long was he there for?"

"He died this morning," growled Steve. "What time did you come to the office?"

"I arrived at nine."

"Not early, like the others?"

"The boss is usually late," I said. "Anyway, you can see

how I wasn't responsible for the murder. I wasn't here until after everyone else."

"But were you the last to leave on Wednesday?"

I thought back. "Er, yes, but I left with Nathan. He can back me up."

"How convenient."

"Look, I have no idea who that dead man is," I said. "Come on, I handed a dangerous criminal over to you just yesterday. Why would I turn around and randomly murder a stranger? I'm not a criminal."

My family might be. I shoved the thought out of mind. What Blythe's mother said didn't matter, and besides, it was irrelevant.

"You have a habit of ending up involved in criminal situations, Blair," said Steve. "It certainly *looks* suspicious from where I'm sitting."

Everything looked suspicious to Steve except for actual criminals.

"I didn't kill him," I said. "Neither did anyone else here today. We only went into Veronica's office to check if she'd left a message on her phone, and there definitely weren't any bodies there."

He grunted. "If I find a connection between you and the victim, then you'll have a lot to answer for, Blair."

"I told you I don't know him. Who is he?"

"None of your concern."

I shifted in the seat. "There's no point in interrogating me when it's clear I have no idea who he is *and* I wasn't here."

Steve wasn't convinced, but after I'd answered the same questions a dozen times, he finally let me go.

"Lizzie Reynolds," Steve called out. "You're next."

Lizzie came out, while I walked into the office to find the two gargoyles standing so close to Veronica that she was trapped in a corner.

"What are you doing?" I asked them.

"I asked the printer to hand me a copy of the victim's file," said the boss, not batting an eyelid at the close proximity of the gargoyles.

"We're in the middle of an investigation," growled Ink Face.

"I thought it might help you to see what information I have on the victim in our files," she said. "Steve isn't exactly the best-honed wand in the drawer, is he?"

"How dare you speak about him like that!" growled Ink Face.

Bethan winced. Being rude to Steve or his fellow gargoyles was usually a bad move, but in fairness to Veronica, she'd only just come out from under the influence of a mind-altering spell and was a little eccentric at the best of times. Unlike her straight-laced daughter, who looked absolutely horrified by the whole thing.

"Uh, maybe check the file later," Bethan said quickly. "Not that it isn't important. I haven't seen Dr Appleton in years, same as you."

"Who is he?" I asked.

The printer made a coughing noise and a wad of paper shot out, hitting me in the nose. I lifted it up. "This guy?"

"That is police property!" said Ink Face.

I gave it a brief scan. Dr Richard Appleton, wizard, former client, professor at the town's only university—

The gargoyle snatched the paper from me. "Enough of that."

"Just looking," I said. "As I told Steve, I have no idea who this man is. So he taught at the university?"

"He did, yes," Veronica said. "Besides, that file isn't police property, it belongs to Eldritch & Co. We have files on everyone we've worked with. It's required."

"Everything in this office is part of the police's investigation," growled Ink Face.

"You can't confiscate our entire office," Bethan protested.

"That sounds like someone who has a secret to hide," Ink Face loomed over Bethan, who took a step backwards.

"Don't be absurd," said Veronica. "Plainly, Dr Appleton broke into my office with a friend and they had an argument. His friend fled when he realised what he'd done."

"You were singing a different song earlier," Ink Face said, his expression stony and his eyes blank. "I heard what you said in your interrogation."

"I'm speculating," Veronica said. "Either the victim was pursued by the murderer here, or the two of them came in at the same time."

"I think it's more likely that he was pursued by the killer," said Bethan. "He ran in here and got hit from behind. It's not like we have security cameras. I think Lizzie was working on that, but it's impossible to design a normal-style camera that works well with the sort of wards Mum uses on her—"

"Enough!" said Ink Face. "Stop speculating. That's the police's job."

"You can't blame us for being curious," I said. "It's not like we have much else to do aside from fixing the printer. How long do we have to stay here?"

"As long as it takes for us to get answers."

"You'll be here all day," said Veronica. "None of us were here when Dr Appleton died. I think the positioning of the body proves that. He fell on me when I opened the office door. If he got in by himself, it's unlikely that there were any witnesses around at that hour in the morning."

"Except for yourself," said Steve, ushering Lizzie back into the office. "I think the person who owns the office is most likely to be the culprit. Especially since you knew the victim." He narrowed his eyes at Veronica.

"I know a lot of people," Veronica said. "Besides, I left town on Monday and came back in the early hours of this morning. And, I reiterate, the man fell on top of me. That means he was killed inside the office. If anything, it's more likely the killer was already in there. Did you check for illusion spells?"

"Nobody was in that office when I got here," Steve snapped. "Callie Rogers, come with me. This won't take long—this murder has a witch's handiwork all over it."

Veronica scowled, while Callie quickly followed him into the reception area. I didn't believe for a minute that Veronica would kill anyone, but with the wards on the office down, anyone might have come here while we'd been gone. Not being a wizard, Steve likely had no idea how to see through illusion spells. Admittedly, neither did I, but still… what if there'd been someone hiding in the office who shouldn't be?

"Did he definitely die when he hit his head?" I asked. "Is that the cause of death?"

"Yes," Ink Face growled. "He fell into the cabinet. Or was pushed."

"Or hit by a spell," Veronica put in.

Ink Face glared at her, his stony gargoyle expression

downright menacing even with inky splatters across his nose. "What do I keep telling you about speculating?"

It was impossible *not* to. At minimum, there'd been two people in the office who shouldn't have been. I was sure it couldn't be a coincidence that it'd happened when the boss had been absent and the wards down, but Veronica's office seemed a bizarre place to commit murder.

"The victim's family has been informed," said Steve, when he returned after questioning Callie. "The body has been taken to the police station for further examination. All of you are to come with me for a more in-depth questioning, until we get to the bottom of this."

Here we go again.

By the time I'd escaped a second grilling, I was exhausted and puzzled beyond measure. This was far from my first interrogation—Steve was admittedly right that I had a knack for ending up involved in these situations more frequently than the average person—but repeating the same questioning twice seemed a colossal waste of time for me as well as the police.

I left the cold, bare-walled interrogation room and walked out into the police station's lobby, which always felt undersized considering it was staffed solely by gargoyles. Nathan stood waiting for me, and the clock above his head told me it was midday. I took a wild guess that we wouldn't be heading back into the office for work this afternoon.

"Hey, Blair," he said. "Sorry about your boss."

"She didn't do it," I said, dropping my voice. "None of us did. We weren't even at the office."

"I know." He folded his arms, a furrow appearing in his brow. "It's odd timing."

"You're telling me. It's like the killer knew we were absent." I stopped in front of him. "Are the police still searching our workplace?"

"I wouldn't advise you to go back, Blair," he said. "If there's a clue there—"

"Steve probably trampled on it." I shook my head, heading for the doors outside. "Come on, you know it's true. The murder weapon could have hit him in the face and he wouldn't have known it."

"It sounds like the victim was sneaked up on from behind," commented Nathan, opening the door to let me leave first. "If there was evidence—footprints or anything —you'd have found it in the reception area."

"The gargoyles rampaged around the whole office." I stepped out into the refreshingly cool summer breeze, more than welcome after the stuffy interrogation room. "Besides, it's not Veronica's doing."

"I know," Nathan said. "She's likely to be allowed to walk away free, considering her link to the victim is tentative at best."

"Good," I said. "We don't need this now, considering how behind we are after she disappeared. Can't say I know what the guy was even looking for."

"Your guess is as good as Steve's. Better, even."

"Ha." I grinned, my mood lifting a little as I fell into step alongside him.

He smiled back. "How'd it go with the elves, anyway?"

"They took the leaves and ran," I said. "The king will get in touch when he feels like it, apparently."

"That seems unfair, after all the trouble you went through to get it."

"Not much I can do," I said. "Anyway, it wasn't all trouble."

Despite the morning I'd had, I remembered our encounter by the falls, crystal clear. And from the look on his face, so did he.

"I have to go and start training some of the new security team," he said. "Unfortunately. But I'll see you later. If I hear anything, I'll let you know, okay?"

I nodded, disappointed that he wasn't sticking around. Then again, he was the town's only full-time security guard. "I didn't know you were training new staff."

"Madame Grey's orders."

That was a good thing. Ever since Peter the wizard had set a monster loose in the woods, there'd been murmurs that the town's security system was less than efficient, and the situation hadn't improved when Blythe's mother had intentionally knocked out several guards to lure three paranormal hunters into town. They'd conspired to bring down the covens and almost succeeded, and I was intensely glad *she'd* been found guilty and jailed.

Nathan and I parted ways on the high street. I very nearly turned around and went back to Dritch & Co, but the sight of more gargoyles heading that way made me pause. If the killer had still been there, hidden by a spell, they'd be long gone by now. Honestly, Steve wouldn't have noticed if an entire contingent of invisible wizards had been having a dance-off right there in the reception through the entire interrogation, but I was sure the killer had taken off long before we'd shown up at the office.

While Veronica's absence had been overshadowed with Madame Grey also falling under the same spell, another mystery we'd never resolved concerned whoever had hired Dritch & Co to contact the paranormal hunters without the permission of the witch covens. Veronica's spell-addled state had meant we'd never found the person responsible. While Veronica herself wasn't on the town council, the company was well respected, and it bothered me that the murderer might taint everything she'd worked to build.

A flash of glitter at my shoulder heralded the arrival of the pixie. Making a chattering noise, it beckoned to me to follow.

"Wait, are we going to the forest?"

The pixie fluttered up and down, waving its hands.

My heart lifted. It looked like I was going to get an audience with the elf king after all.

3

Sure enough, the same elf who'd visited me that morning met me at the entrance to the forest path, not far from the house where old Ava the seer's granddaughter lived. With barely a nod, he turned down the woodland path and darted away. He moved fast considering the tangled undergrowth, and I had to run to keep up without losing sight of him.

I made a valiant effort to memorise the route so I wouldn't end up lost on shifter territory on the way back like last time, but the deeper part of the forest seemed designed to confuse anyone who walked in. The path dipped and wove around ancient trees and valleys of bright flowering plants I was sure I'd never seen growing in regular forests. Nor was the presence of hundreds of elves watching us from the bushes, wielding sharpened branches.

The elf king's home was inside a giant hollow tree, whose sprawling roots covered a huge section of the forest floor. I followed the elf guard inside, this time undoing my own glamour. With a snap of my fingers, I was in fairy mode. Too bad it didn't make climbing into a tunnel built for people under five feet tall any less awkward. I crawled at a half-crouch until we reached the place where the tunnel became a cave. The elven king sat on a tree stump set up to resemble a throne, and the only visible difference between him and his subjects was the gold leaf detail on his bark-coloured clothes.

"Blair Wilkes." He held up the handful of pixie dust in his hand.

"Ah, hello, your Majesty," I said. "As you can see, I found what you asked me to."

"Yes, you did," he said. "You passed the test."

I waited expectantly. "You said you'd tell me more about what my dad was doing in the woods the last time you saw him."

"Patience, fairy," said the elf king. "Do you know what this is?"

"Er, pixie dust? It was supposed to be extinct…"

"It can only be brought back to life by a fairy's touch. Your father left it there, Blair."

My heart jumped in my chest. "My dad. You met him?"

"It was four or five years ago," said the elf king. "A terrible winter even by human standards. The whole forest was blanketed in snow. Our trees froze. And one night, a man appeared in the woods. At first he pretended to be human, but we saw through his glamour, and hauled him in for questioning as we would any trespasser." He paused for a moment. "The man begged for shelter for a single night. He told us he was being pursued by a terrible foe, but that he wouldn't disturb us for long. He stayed that night and said little except that his life was in danger.

In the morning, he was gone. Not long after, we heard that he'd been caught by those murderous hunters and jailed."

My head hit the ceiling. I'd accidentally beat my wings without meaning to. *Pursued by a terrible foe?* "So my dad was running from someone? Who?"

"He refused to tell us," said the elven king. "That is all I can tell you, Blair Wilkes."

Your parents were common thieves, said Blythe's mother. And yet that wasn't the worst of it. What was chasing my dad, something that'd scared him into avoiding me for almost my entire life?

"He… didn't mention my mother, did he?" I asked, my voice higher than usual.

"He mentioned a child."

My throat closed up. "What… what did he say?"

"He said that any child of his would be able to find the pixie dust he left behind the falls."

"And…"

"And that is all, Blair Wilkes."

I don't understand. My imagination went into overdrive imagining what might have driven my father to hide out here in the forest. He thought my life was in danger, too?

The elves seemed relieved to be rid of me when I left their abode. I barely paid attention to where I walked. All those stories I'd made up when I was a kid about my parents fighting crime Batman-style took on a whole new meaning. How was I supposed to talk to my dad before the winter solstice, the next time he'd be allowed a supervised visit outside the jail? I didn't even know where the Lancashire Prison for Paranormals was. Nathan had implied the branch of hunters his family ran wasn't too far from the town, but he'd also said it was divided into different departments. High-security prisons weren't the same branch as whoever ran the independent hunters whose job involved killing rogue shifters who attacked humans or arresting magical serial killers.

Speaking of shifters, I'd better get away from their territory otherwise I'd get hauled in as a trespasser. Being arrested once in a day was more than enough for me. As a fairy, I could move faster, flitting through the branches. I'd barely scratched the surface of fairy magic. The pixie could do more than me, including appearing from thin air and turning invisible. Now that would come in handy. Definitely better than my one disastrous attempt at making an invisibility potion, in which I'd wound up turning transparent instead. Maybe that was a safe topic to ask my dad about...

Half an hour of flying in circles later, I tracked down the way out of the woods. The shifters or elves really needed to invest in signposting. At least I'd killed some time, since going back to work wasn't an option. Alissa would be home now, so I turned into my human form again and walked back to the flat.

Alissa looked up from the heavy medical textbook she was reading when I walked into the living room. "Hey, Blair. You're early. Did your boss take pity on you and let you have a long weekend?"

"No, she's been accused of murdering a guy who we found inside her office." I sank into the armchair, since the cats occupied the rest of the sofa.

"Murdering someone in her office?" She put down her book. "Oh, no. Who?"

"Someone called Dr Appleton," I said. "A professor at

the university. Nobody set foot in the office after Wednesday, but Steve's using his normal level of finesse and has decided Veronica's guilty by default."

"He would." Alissa frowned. "I haven't heard from Bethan."

"She's helping her mum," I said. "It's been chaos. The police questioned everyone, the printer threw a tantrum, and it's pretty clear none of us was around when the guy died, however it happened. But the wards stopped working when Veronica took off. Her memory of everything that happened since she got hit by Blythe's sister's magic is fuzzy."

"Oh, no. You never seem to catch a break, do you?"

"You're telling me." I leaned forward to pet Sky. "I hope my magic lesson is going ahead."

"It should be, since the meeting's over," said Alissa. "I wondered if you'd heard they voted yes."

"Voted yes?" I said blankly.

"Er, the council?" she said. "You know. Big meeting today, remember? They voted yes on the decision to hire more security from outside the town, in addition to the people Madame Grey nominated."

I'd forgotten the council was supposed to be meeting today to vote on whether or not to bring in external security to guard the town's borders. Since they'd already had a meeting yesterday and I'd had such an eventful day already, it'd slipped my mind.

"So they voted yes on bringing people to town who don't live here?" I asked. "I thought... I thought since Blythe's mum's in jail and she got caught..."

"It's not necessarily going to be the hunters," said Alissa. "Just anyone from outside the town with experience in paranormal security. I imagine they'll go through Dritch & Co… ah."

"Yeah, exactly," I said, my heart sinking. "We never did find out who slipped the hunters' info into our files to begin with. Nathan said the hunters claimed they got the call inviting them to apply from someone called Mrs Johnson, but that might have been Mrs Dailey using an alias, or one of her friends."

Alissa bit her lip. "Maybe. I think they'll just ask paranormal security guards from the surrounding towns to come in. That's easier. But I don't know how they'll do it without Dritch & Co."

"Me neither." It wasn't the idea of inviting other paranormals here that bothered me—our company interviewed clients from outside the town all the time. But with Veronica a murder suspect, conducting interviews might be tricky—and the only people who *didn't* need to apply through Dritch & Co were the paranormal hunters.

"Blair, why are there leaves in your hair?" Alissa asked.

"I took an unplanned detour via the elf king's place on the way back from the police station."

I leaned forward in the armchair, giving Sky another stroke, and told Alissa what I'd learned.

Her eyes rounded. "They met your dad. That's… wow. What are you going to do now?"

"I already wrote to him today." I slumped back against the cushions. "I guess being chased by someone dangerous is a good enough reason for him not to have got in touch with me. I just hoped for something a bit more specific. I know I shouldn't have expected to learn anything at all…"

"It's not your fault, Blair," she said sympathetically.

"You know he wants to get to know you now, and you have a way of keeping in contact."

True. Having to go through the pixie and not being able to say anything important might be frustrating, but it was better than the alternative. "I should be more worried about my job. Veronica didn't say if there's any point in coming back to work on Monday. Since the place is under investigation for murder... wait, shouldn't Madame Grey be involved?"

"She would have been if she hadn't been presiding over the council meeting," said Alissa. "I expect she'll be at the police station now, if I know her."

"She'll get Veronica off the hook." *I hope.* "You know, I don't think I've ever had the chance to talk to her about my magic. Not that I'm a priority, but you know, I'm starting to think I'll never have time to complete my witch training."

"I'm sure your lesson tonight will go ahead as usual," said Alissa. "Pretty sure Rita tells Madame Grey everything, but since she spent half the week in a coffin, she might be a bit behind."

"Would you believe I forgot about the coffin thing?" I shook my head. "Poor Rebecca might have to wait a while for her training to start, if the witches have to run around accommodating new security guards. I can't believe they voted yes."

I'd really hoped that Blythe's mother was in the minority, but of course, others had agreed with her when she'd suggested replacing the current coven system with something new. I couldn't claim to be an expert on how the whole thing worked, but the Meadowsweet Coven owned the town, making its leader the person in charge. Each of the other covens nominated a leader to serve on the council, no matter how small, and there were representatives from the vampires, shifters and other paranormal groups, too. Mrs Dailey had shaken things up when she'd argued for bringing in an outside committee to run the town instead. Specifically, the paranormal hunters. At least *that* wasn't going ahead, but I didn't like to think what would have happened if we'd failed to find Madame Grey in time for her to put a stop to it.

"Me neither," said Alissa, picking up her textbook again. "Want me to help you study? I'm taking a summer class in advanced healing, but reading this thing is tedious work."

"At least you can use a basic healing spell. I gave myself a nosebleed last time." I was weeks behind on lessons and I'd started at a huge disadvantage already, since most witches learned magic from childhood. No amount of latent talent would make up for my shoddy technique, and the best magic I'd done was when I'd imitated someone else's spells in a crisis. That proved I had inherited at least a little of my mother's skill, though, and I hoped the rest would come in time.

———

Rita, my magic tutor, waited for me in the classroom at the witches' headquarters. The diviner was in her forties and had long curly hair dyed in red streaks, while she wore a large number of bangles on both wrists. Her wand was decorated in a similar manner, making my own wand —embellished with a pair of fairy wings—look plain by comparison.

"Hey, Rita." I reached my usual desk at the front of the classroom and put my bag down. "I wasn't sure what we were doing today, so I looked at the next chapter in the textbook."

"I heard about what happened at your workplace," said Rita, sending all thoughts of theory work fleeing from my head.

"Ah," I said. "Yeah, Steve's being ridiculous. I know Veronica wouldn't have killed anyone. She wasn't even back in town until early this morning, for a start."

"No, it sounds like the victim was unfortunate enough to be trespassing at the wrong time," she said. "I only heard the story second-hand, mind."

"So you didn't know Dr Appleton?"

She shook her head. "I do tutor at the academy, but not at the university. Do the police have any other suspects?"

"Nobody was around but us," I said. "Steve just seemed to want to blame Veronica, or me. He barely looked at the actual crime scene. Has Madame Grey been there?"

"Yes, but she found nothing of note," she said. "It's very difficult to solve a magical crime of that sort with no witnesses, because magic often leaves no traces. It's not uncommon for crimes here to go unresolved, but Steve feels he needs to have a result each time."

"Yeah. I mean, look at what Rebecca did." Blythe's younger sister had turned people's personalities inside-out without leaving a single visible sign. "It seems weird that the professor broke into our workplace. What might he have been looking for in there?"

"Anything," said Rita. "I'm afraid I didn't know him, so I can't comment on his motives. It seems he took advantage of Veronica's absence and tried to sneak into her office. I'm sure Steve will come to his senses in time."

He was more likely to take up ballet dancing than give in, but rehashing the murder wouldn't help me be a better witch. I pulled out my textbook. "Okay. Are we going to do theory work?"

She eyed the wand sticking out of my pocket. "I heard you learned some new spells lately. Let's see a demonstration first."

Typical Rita—direct and to the point. I picked up my wand, and began.

———

I got through the lesson without dyeing anything purple or starting a fire, which had once been a tall order. Once Rita had checked my technique was fine on the new spells I'd learned, she'd had me return to theory work for the last portion of the lesson.

"You might be ready for your next round of assessments soon," Rita said. "If you can learn all the material over the summer. However, Madame Grey is in charge of scheduling the exams, so it might be a while before she can fit you in. Unless you want to be assessed with the students at the academy."

"I think I'd rather take the test alone."

Rita gave me a stern look. "You'll have to join a class when you start learning the type of spells which require practising with a partner. Theory you can do alone, but you can't learn everything through improvisation."

"Oh," I said. "Yeah. I know. Just… I'm not sure I'm ready for another person to be involved in my magic lessons yet." I wasn't yet confident that I'd moved past the 'accident-prone to the point of utter disaster' phase.

"You're on Grade Two theory-wise," she said. "As far as practical skills go, you've used a number of spells that are far beyond your level, but you lack the theoretical foundation to be tested on them. That said, I think the testing levels have their limits, and when you were in life-threatening situations, you can hardly be blamed for defending yourself. The transportation spell you copied from Madame Grey a few weeks ago, however, is very much beyond your level. You're lucky it didn't go horribly wrong."

"Mm." I'd dyed the classroom purple enough times that I didn't blame Rita for being sceptical. In addition to transportation spells, I'd undone advanced wards by imitating Madame Grey, and inadvertently cast several spells which I wasn't sure were even in the textbook, like creating a luminous disco ball in the middle of the flat. Alissa had also taught me a few practical basics, like the drying spell. "I'll try to only do that if it's urgent."

"Your fairy magic is a whole other matter," said Rita. "Have you learned any more about what you can do?"

"I can undo and redo my glamour whenever I like now," I said. "It turns out that I'm left-wand-handed because my fairy magic works best in my right hand. Or maybe the other way around." I snapped my fingers in demonstration, turning into a fairy and then into a witch again.

"Good," she said. "I'm afraid there's no formal assessment for fairy magic, but if you want to continue to represent the fairies at council meetings, you'll have to be consistent about it. The others were questioning why you weren't there today."

"Ah. I didn't know I had to come to every meeting. But —if I'd been there, would I have been able to stop them from voting in favour of bringing the hunters in?"

"Nobody mentioned bringing the hunters in, Blair."

"I thought it was implied," I said. "Right? They wanted to become our new security. They were on the list at Dritch & Co… before our office shut down, anyway. What's going to happen with that?"

"If the police let Veronica go without further questioning, it's likely that Madame Grey will request that the hiring process goes ahead as planned. It was Veronica who had all the relevant information on the potential candidates to join our new security team."

"I did wonder," I admitted. "We were supposed to be inviting people in for interviews this week, but the notes got jumbled when Veronica disappeared. But—the hunters' contact details were definitely there. It seems weird that someone would tell us to call them in without consulting Madame Grey first."

Before Rita could respond, the door opened and the woman herself entered the classroom. Madame Grey was even more imposing than Rita, with white hair grown past her shoulders, and grey attire that gave her a regal, almost queenly cast. She peered at me through silver-rimmed glasses.

"Hey, Madame Grey," I said, my heart leaping. I'd been desperate to discuss my magic with her for weeks, but ever since the werewolves and vampires had almost started a war over the murders committed by Peter the wizard, it'd been incredibly hard to get hold of the town's leader. As soon as the conflict was over, she'd been hit by Rebecca's spell and taken up sleeping in one of the vampires' coffins. Not that you'd ever believe a woman so formidable would ever do anything that undignified.

"I wanted a word with you, Blair," she said.

About what? My magic lessons? The elves? Veronica? My cat? Anyone's guess.

"Oh, sure," I said. "Is it about my magic?"

"Blair, were you aware that someone passed on the hunters' details to your workplace?" she asked.

I blinked. That, I hadn't seen coming. "Yes," I said. "I thought it was odd at the time, but I trusted Veronica's expertise, before she was put under a spell. Why?"

"I found the files in Veronica's office," she explained. "I thought something seemed out of place, and checked with my own records. I normally vet anyone who wants to hire Veronica and check the details before handing them to her, at her own request. But the information of the hunters' branch appears to have been slipped into the files at some point before it turned up in your office on Monday."

"I... really?" I'd wondered if I was being paranoid, thinking someone had *wanted* us to call the hunters behind Madame Grey's back. Maybe it was true after all.

"Yes," she said. "She gave you the files herself?"

"She was distracted at the time," I said. "We didn't know she was under a spell. Even Rebecca... I don't think it was her doing."

"Don't worry, nothing will happen to Rebecca," she said. "But I'm concerned about who slipped that file in. They must have done so before I handed it to her."

"While you were under the spell?"

"No. Before."

That's not good. "You think another witch did it." Blythe's mother was the obvious example, but there were others who'd supported her.

"The rest of the council denied it," she said. "Naturally. Did you speak to the hunters in person?"

"Oh, when they called the office? No. I left a message, and when they called back, Callie shifted. You probably heard that part. But I thought Nathan ordered them to leave."

"Yes, he did," she said. "Which is why I was surprised to get a call from them this morning. It seems the town's on a watchlist."

My heart lurched. "Really? What does that mean?"

"It means they'll be back to make my life difficult," said Madame Grey. "Certainly nothing I haven't handled before."

I wished I had her confidence. "But—some of the hunters were invited here by Blythe's mother," I said. "They worked together. You… you think she slipped that file in, right?"

Her expression was grave. "It cannot be proved, but what's done is done."

"Is there anything I can do to help?"

Madame Grey's glasses flashed under the light as she dipped her head. "Yes, Blair, there is. Veronica will need to stay on the police's good side if she's to hire the town's new security team. And you'll be helping her. I'm sure I can trust you to pick the right people."

"Me?" My voice squeaked. Sure, it was my job to interview clients, but Veronica was the one with the expertise.

On the other hand… "You want me to vet them with my lie-sensing power."

Oh. My power would ensure I chose people who were right for the position and had no ties to the hunters. That's why she needed me.

No pressure, Blair.

"What about the murder?" I asked. "Did you know the victim?"

"Not well," she said. "Do be careful, Blair. Security is more important than ever."

She left the room, while I remained still. Madame Grey had trusted me with the interviewing process to hire the town's new security team. Admittedly, I was meant to be doing that anyway, but after today, my confidence was a little shaky. How was I supposed to adequately assess who would be good at defending the town if there'd been a major security breach right there in the office—one that had resulted in a man's death? Even if it was none of my business, the last time someone had broken into the place, it'd had Blythe written all over it. And I had the suspicion her family wasn't finished with me yet.

4

I went to work on Monday with the resolve to do as good a job as possible and not let Madame Grey down. Alissa and I had spent a relaxing weekend by the lake, practising magic and watching the High Fliers perform outrageous stunts above the water. Luckily, she no longer had any desire to join them up in the air, and I felt more confident in my decisions knowing I'd at least managed to put that right.

I'd called my foster parents, too, which had been trickier. Knowing I was deceiving them about being in contact with my dad weighed heavily on my mind, but the alternative was letting them in on the paranormal world—which was forbidden. Since Mr and Mrs Wilkes were still enjoying their retirement in Australia, I'd yet to face the decision of whether to tell them the truth about my new job, let alone the rest of it. I hadn't heard from Nathan either, though that wasn't so unusual, given that he'd been training the new security team. Now it was up to me to interview the rest.

Callie waved at me as I entered Dritch & Co's office. Her desk looked sparser than usual, and the papers that Veronica had left in the corner had also gone.

"Did the police take everything?" I asked.

"Yes," she said. "It's been a nightmare. I offered to work through the weekend and help duplicate the files that were involved in the mix-up, but half of them had to be thrown out. Veronica tried to redo the rest, but only after she got them back from the police."

"That means we'll be behind for weeks," I surmised. "Veronica does know I'm running interviews for new security guards, right?"

"You'll have to ask her," she said, shuffling papers. "She's incredibly displeased with the mess Steve made."

"He hasn't called Veronica in for another questioning, right?" I asked, heading for the office door. "Or have the police found any other suspects?"

"Last I heard, they were talking to the victim's family," she said.

Oh, right. "I hope they find who did it." For all our sakes.

I entered the office to find Veronica and Bethan in conversation, while Lizzie fiddled with the printer. I quickly sat down behind the computer to avoid any more potential ink projectiles.

"Blair," said Veronica, turning to me. "Since you've already called some potential security candidates, that's your task for today. It's a priority, considering the current situation."

"Sure," I said. "Are, er, the police okay with us doing the interviews here, considering their investigation?"

"They haven't said otherwise."

From Steve, that was the best we'd get.

When Veronica left, I immediately dove into work. Time was of the essence, and Madame Grey was counting on me.

Bethan moved like a human whirlwind, too. I strongly suspected she'd helped her mother reorganise the files so quickly, because her magical talent was of a similar type. She and Lizzie handled the calls and emails for the day, but I did most of the interviewing. Not because I was particularly good at it, but because of my lie-sensing power. No hunters would make it through—I'd be sure of it.

By afternoon, I'd referred a dozen people to Madame Grey for further interviews and felt reasonably confident that we'd have enough people by the end of the week to cover every inch of the town's borders. The candidates included a wizard who claimed to be the best at defensive spells in the north of England. I'd asked for a demonstration, then regretted it when he'd knocked everyone in the office out of their seats at the same time and accidentally caused the printer to throw another tantrum. I'd also referred a couple of vampires, including Alissa's ex, Keith. The elder vampires had enough money that they'd never have to work another day in their eternal lives, so there was zero chance of any of them stepping in to help, but the younger vampires were eager, swift and deadly. Barely any candidates lied on their applications, but the requirements were low. The most important trait was the ability to stand one's ground and demonstrate basic level-headedness under pressure. A low bar, but some still failed, including a goblin who spent the entire interview telling me an anecdote about a prank he and his friends had played on an unsuspecting gargoyle involving a halo and a lot of glitter. When I asked for a demonstration of his experience in defence, he'd fainted when Bethan had used a basic attack spell on him.

"Probably for the best," she said, putting her wand away. "Goblins have two modes when it comes to defence, 'run and hide' or 'bite the enemy's fingers off'. We don't need either of those things from security guards."

"You might have warned me." I woke the unconscious goblin with a revival spell and dismissed him. "You'd think trolls would be good security guards."

"They sleep half the time and can't distinguish between friend and foe when they're tired," said Lizzie.

Maybe not then. I sat down and sent a few more emails, pleased with the progress I'd made. I hadn't even needed to call any of the out-of-town candidates yet.

"Hey, someone's here to see you," said Bethan.

I turned to the window and spotted Nathan outside. "At this time? Pretty sure he's here to see the boss."

"And you as a bonus."

"What, you think he wants me to interview him?" I shuffled the papers. "Nah, if anything, he'll be the one doing the interviewing. Madame Grey has him training the new team after she's done with them."

The office door opened a minute later, and Nathan came in.

"Hey, Blair," he said. "I wanted to check who you'd interviewed for the security position today."

"Sure." I gave him the details. "Don't worry, I thoroughly questioned all of them."

"Just making sure," he said. "It seems the pack chief has been telling people not to apply here."

"Seriously? I guess that's why none of the shifter candidates responded to my emails." Chief Donovan's grudge against me would have doubled in size after his daughter had got caught in Rebecca's spell, so I should have seen it coming. It was a shame, though, given that shifters were great at defending their territory. At least they already had full control of the forest's northwest border.

"That, and I'm doing the third interview round," Nathan said. "Even the shifters who don't like Donovan won't work with the hunters."

"You're not one," I said. "I guess arguing with the chief is like trying to put a halo on Steve and turn him into a Christmas decoration."

"Did you interview a goblin named Rod, by any chance?"

"You know him?"

"I had to help the police find the goblins responsible after that incident."

I grinned. "Don't worry, he failed the interview. I don't think Steve and the gargoyles need pranksters on the team." Though it might liven them up a bit.

"Madame Grey sent me to check up on you, but it looks like you've got it all in hand." He returned the papers to my desk.

"Oh, you spoke to her?" I asked. "Does she know who might have referred the hunters to us, or is it officially blamed on Mrs Dailey?"

Bethan and Lizzie looked curiously at me.

"No," he said. "She doesn't. Nor have we found who this Mrs Johnson person was."

"Who?" asked Bethan.

"The person who called the hunters telling them to apply to work with us," I explained. "They bypassed Madame Grey and slipped their details into the files without anyone noticing. I'm taking a wild guess it was Blythe's mother using an alias, but there's a chance it might have been someone else."

"Oh," said Bethan, exchanging a concerned look with Lizzie. "Yeah, that does sound fishy. But she's in jail. It doesn't really matter now."

"It matters because the hunters are back," said Nathan. "It seems they want to conduct their meeting with Madame Grey in person."

"She mentioned that yesterday," I said, though my heart sank to hear it confirmed. Barely days had passed since the vote and the hunters were already taking matters into their own hands? Madame Grey didn't suffer fools, but the hunters were worryingly persistent considering we'd send them packing just last week.

"I'm glad to hear you found some good candidates, Blair," he said seriously. "We'll need them. I'm going to speak to Veronica, but I'll be around later."

"See you in a bit."

He left the office, and I turned back to the others.

"He wasn't just making up excuses to see me," I said. "This is serious. The last group of hunters who came here… let's just say it was a really good job Nathan chased them off. They were working with Mrs Dailey."

"Ugh," said Bethan. "Did she really slip the hunters' info into our files?"

"Either her, or someone acting on her orders," I said. "It's lucky we got to go ahead with the hiring process at all."

"No kidding," said Bethan. "It's *not* lucky that we're still one member short. I don't know how Veronica's going to find time to hire anyone else while we're in the middle of this mess. Lena said she's never coming back to town again."

I grimaced. Who'd want to work in an office where the boss had been accused of murder? Especially with the hunters running around causing trouble?

———

Despite a second round of successful interviews, I ended the day feeling like I hadn't done enough. The thought that someone had used Dritch & Co to get the hunters to come to town remained in the back of my mind, along with the reminder that they were coming to send people to talk to Madame Grey. Even if they sent their most qualified team rather than the three dunces Mrs Dailey had invited, their renewed interest in Fairy Falls had her fingerprints all over it.

Nathan waited for me outside the doors, and I did my best to smile at him. "I sent more people your way, if you'd like a list."

"It's okay, I trust you," he said, and I warmed all over. "I'll start the interviews when Madame Grey's done with them."

"Good. We could only test basic spells in the office and even then, two wizards nearly set the place on fire."

"Ah," he said. "Yes, I'd have suggested leaving the practical tests to Madame Grey. Though double-checking their skills is never a bad thing."

"It was a way to double-check they were definitely

paranormals, too," I said. "Not that I thought the hunters would send someone in disguised as a wizard, but you never know."

"The hunters would likely apply under their own names, but you were right to be cautious," he said.

"But they're still coming to speak to Madame Grey," I said. "I really don't understand why. She's the person in charge, not them."

"They write the law, unfortunately," he said. "All paranormal law in the region ultimately comes from them. They frequently inspect any town on their list as high-risk—frankly, I'm surprised it took us this long to draw their attention."

"Like the paranormal Ofsted?" I asked. In response to his blank expression, I added, "School inspectors in the normal world."

"I suppose," he said. "Once they see we have adequate security in place, they'll take off."

"Aren't the gargoyles enough? I mean, from an outsider's perspective, if I heard a town was guarded by terrifying gargoyles, I'd assume it was pretty safe."

"That's probably why they've left us alone until now," he commented. "That, and I gave them frequent reports via my family. I suppose they thought my own presence was enough, but when the incident last week happened, someone went straight to the higher-ups."

"Mrs Dailey," I said immediately. "She set up things so that Dritch & Co would be the ones to call the hunters, too."

"Yes," he said. "There's nothing she can do from behind bars, though."

"I don't trust her." Major understatement. "What will happen if the hunters decide we aren't up to scratch?"

"They'll replace all the security with a team of their own, for a start, and Madame Grey and the council will be replaced by a new committee."

"That was exactly what Mrs Dailey wanted," I said. "I just hope the others won't stand for it."

"Mostly, it's the effect on the other paranormals that worries me," he said. "Our town has relatively little conflict because the different paranormals generally don't go out of their way to antagonise one another. The hunters can never resist telling people who's boss, which won't go down well with the shifters, for one."

"I can imagine how Chief Donovan would react to that," I said. "Considering he already told his people to avoid me. And you."

"I expected nothing less," he said. "I have to admit, I also came here to make sure Steve wasn't giving you any trouble."

"About the murder?" I asked. "Did Steve mention keeping the investigation open? Has he questioned anyone else?"

"He's spoken to the victim's family and put an open invitation to anyone with information to come forward," he said. "I wouldn't advise you to ask him in person. Steve didn't take the news of outsiders coming in well, and he's currently storming around yelling at everyone in his office."

"Of course he wouldn't like it, since the implication is that he isn't doing his job." I rolled my eyes. "All right, I'll stay put. It's not like I enjoy talking to the guy. Though I'd pay to see him wearing a halo."

Nathan smiled. "Believe me, I wish I'd seen more than the aftermath. I have to go and speak to Madame Grey now, but I'll take you out for dinner after your lesson."

"That'd be great." Better than great. We had a shot at a relationship, and nobody—hunters, Steve, or my jailed nemesis—was going to spoil it.

———

It took great effort to keep from skipping to the witches' headquarters an hour later. When I walked into the classroom for my lesson, I found Rebecca sat next to my usual spot with Rita in front of her. "Oh. Am I interrupting?"

"Not at all," said Rita. "Since you two are both beginners, I thought you might be able to help Rebecca out, Blair."

"Er, okay." I'd wondered how Rebecca had been getting along. Since her mother had been jailed, I'd heard another witch family had taken her in, since her dad lived outside of the town and she needed to start her magical training immediately.

"We were intending to start with the basics of Rebecca's power," she said. "Testing the limits, that type of thing. It's harder for some witches than others. Your power, for instance, doesn't seem to be affected by distance, but you'd already had experience in using it consciously before showing up here."

I wouldn't say I used it consciously. Accidentally was more like it. Rebecca was the same, except her ability to affect people's personalities was far more dangerous than my own power when left unchecked. Madame Grey was likely too busy to assign her a tutor in person, which I understood, given the number of other responsibilities on her hands. But I was definitely not qualified to train anyone. I barely had a handle on my own magic at the best of times.

"My power only works on people I make eye contact with," Rebecca said. "I'm told that's common."

"Very common when it comes to mind powers," said Rita.

"Except mind reading," I said. Blythe didn't need eye contact to read my mind, but I hadn't met many other witches or wizards with psychic powers. Aside from Blythe and her mother, the only other one I'd met was the killer Simeon Clarke, who had mind control powers and the ability to erase memories.

Rebecca looked at me. "Uh, mind reading works on you, doesn't it?"

"Usually. I think. Why?"

"I don't think my power works on you," she said. "I mean, I don't use it on purpose, but last week, it was hitting everyone in sight."

"Wait, it doesn't?" I frowned. "Not at all?"

"No. I looked you in the eye plenty of times and you were fine. Weird."

"Not really," said Rita. "Blair's been known to block other psychics' powers on occasion."

Like when Mrs Dailey tried to break into my mind and erase my memories. Goosebumps rose on my arms at the reminder of what a close call I'd had.

"I did wonder why everyone who came into contact with you was affected except me," I admitted, "but I thought you didn't try to use your power on me."

"No, I did," she said. "Not deliberately, but you know, it affected everyone I went near. I think you're immune."

"Precisely why I wanted to ask you to help out," said Rita, moving towards the door. "See if you can break Blair's defences, Rebecca. That should keep you busy for a while."

"Hang on," said Rebecca, but the door swung shut behind the older witch. "Is that it?"

"That's her training style," I said. "Throw you in the deep end. Except when it comes to wand-work, that is. Then she makes you practise until your arm falls off." I closed my mouth before I gave her too much of a fright. "Anyway, try using your power on me."

I looked directly into her eyes. Her brow furrowed in concentration. "I'm using my power. I think."

"Nothing happening here," I responded. "I don't know if I'm totally immune. Maybe it's because my powers are a type of mind-magic, too."

"Are they?" Rebecca looked away, then met my gaze again. "I knew you were a fairy, but... can you read minds?"

"No," I said. "I can tell what type of paranormal someone is when I look at them or hear their voice, even if they haven't told me. But that might be my fairy power, not a witch one. I can also tell if someone's lying or not. It's to do with being able to sense the truth of a person...apparently."

"Wow," she said. "That's *awesome.*"

"I guess it is," I admitted. "I also blocked a vampire or two from reading my mind, by accident."

"Really?" she asked. "Maybe that's what you're doing.

Blocking me. You can block other witches with similar powers. But not my—not my mum."

"I did in the end," I said. When she'd tried to force her way into my mind, and I'd barely been conscious of doing it. "Maybe it's because we're relat—" I broke off.

Rebecca blinked. "Because we're what?"

"Uh. Nothing."

"Related," she said. "Who, you and me? Or Blythe?"

"It was a rumour I heard," I said, wishing I hadn't said anything. "Because our abilities are similar, my friend thought Blythe and I were maybe second cousins. She knew my mum when they were kids."

"She never told *me* that," said Rebecca. "Blythe doesn't talk to me much anyway, and Mum… all she ever did was talk about how the covens were plotting against her."

"You didn't always live in Fairy Falls, right?" I asked. "You moved here recently."

"I did when I was younger. Then my mum got married again, so we moved, but we came back here last year. Then Blythe came back to live with us."

"Yeah, when she got fired from Dritch & Co," I said. "Did your mum ever mention my boss, Veronica Eldritch? Or your sister?"

"No," said Rebecca. "Why?"

"Nothing." I shook my head. I didn't need to share my theories with her. Mrs Dailey had given her enough grief already. "Who's looking after you now?"

"I'm living with Mrs Farrington. She's nice."

"Good," I said, glad they hadn't pressured Blythe to take care of her. From Rebecca's wary expression, the mention of her mother had put her on the defensive. "Try to use your ability on me again."

Several rounds of practise later, it became apparent that I *was* immune to Rebecca's power, with no obvious exceptions.

"How's it going?" asked Rita, re-entering the classroom.

"She can't affect me at all," I said. "Not with eye contact or otherwise."

"Really?" she said. "Interesting. I'll inform Madame Grey. Rebecca, you might have to find someone else to test your limits on, but I think we have enough information to start off your training. I'll set you up with the theory books and if you're lucky, you'll have a wand by the summer's end."

Rebecca's face lit up. "A wand?"

"Blair, I'll redo your schedule," Rita added. "But you'll need to start studying if you want to take the second level theory test and your first wand examination before the academy's summer schools take over the schedule."

"The academies have the same holidays as the humans, then?" I asked, my heart flipping uneasily at the prospect of more exams. I'd been lucky to pass the last one.

"Yes," she said. "If you like, you can sign up to a summer class. Some of our more ambitious pupils do that. However, if you do, you'll need to learn to work with a partner. It's required."

"Oh. Right." I couldn't fight it forever, but most beginner witches were five years old. I'd already accidentally turned Madame Grey's tween granddaughter transparent and received a tongue-lashing for it. I didn't want to spend the rest of the summer hiding from disgruntled parents for turning their offspring blue or invisible.

After Rita had assigned me a pile of reading, I left the

room, while Rebecca stayed behind to discuss her training in more depth. On the way out of the witches' headquarters, I ran into Nina, my neighbour. She was tall and curvy and had vibrant strawberry blond hair.

"Oh, hey, Nina," I said. I still felt kind of bad for suspecting her of being responsible for the personality-altering curse due to her animosity towards Blythe. "Here for a magic lesson?"

"No, I'm here to speak to Madame Grey. Coven business."

"Ah." From what she'd told me, her mother and herself were in the process of setting up their own coven after leaving the Nightshade Coven following an argument between her mother and their leader. "Going well, then?"

"Better than before," she said. "I mean better than… you know. Before she was jailed." *Oh.* I'd forgotten that Mrs Dailey had been blackmailing her mother in some way.

"Glad to hear it," I said. "I think Madame Grey's in her office, if she's done with the interviews."

"Security?" she asked. "I heard you're being pressured to find the new security team."

"Not really pressured," I said. Most of the pressure, I'd added myself, because I didn't want to let Madame Grey down. "I found quite a few people today."

Puzzlement crossed her features. "Oh, I thought…"

"Thought what?" I said.

She gave a vigorous head shake. "Nothing. I mean, the murder. We heard all about it because the man who died used to be married to a council member."

"Wait, he was? Who?"

Her gaze dropped. "He was married to Azalea, the leader of the Nightshade Coven. My old coven."

"Madame Grey didn't mention that." She'd said she hadn't known him well, but did that change things? It wasn't like I knew who the police had questioned after they'd eventually let Veronica go.

"Well, they divorced a while ago," she said. "So your boss is off the hook?"

"Last I heard," I said. "The police questioned all of us, but hopefully they'll catch who really did it."

"Yeah, I hope so. See you later, Blair."

I stood still for a moment, taking in the new information. The murder victim had been married to a coven leader? The investigation wasn't any of my business, but...

"Hey. Blair." Nathan stepped in front of me. "You were miles away. Something wrong?"

"Nope," I said. "Just thinking about my lesson. Rita had me help Rebecca out today."

I told him about my lesson while we walked to the Troll's Tavern. Nathan held my hand all the way there, seemingly oblivious to the stares. There seemed to be more people around than usual, and I did my best not to cringe away from the attention. A fairy dating an ex-hunter surely wasn't *that* much of a novelty.

The Troll's Tavern was packed. There was some kind of end-of-term celebration at the academy, so the place was rammed with underage witches and wizards trying to sneakily order cocktails. Nathan and I were instantly surrounded by rowdy students, and when we tried to get to our usual table, we found Leopold, the inept graduate who'd had zero luck in the job department, sitting there.

"Hey, Blair," he said, looking morose.

"Hey, no luck with work?"

He grunted. "Nope."

"You're welcome to apply to be part of the town's security force," I said, though I doubted he'd get through an interview. He hadn't fared particularly well at being Mr Falconer's assistant, and as it'd been a while since I'd seen him sober, he wouldn't be much help at deterring trespassers.

Nathan and I found a free table and ordered meals and drinks, but we could barely hear ourselves talk. I hadn't told him about my latest encounter with the elf king yet, but people kept 'accidentally' wandering closer to our table to stare at the fairy and the hunter. I gave up trying to ignore them and suggested we leave. Nathan agreed, and we made our way through the crowd to the door. Leopold was apparently fed up with drowning his sorrows, too, because he left the pub at the same time, nearly falling over his own feet on the way out. Then he recovered and teetered off into an alleyway.

"That's a dead end," Nathan remarked. "What's he doing?"

I shook my head. "Who even knows why Leopold does whatever he does? At least Blythe wasn't there this time."

"You haven't seen her since the spell came off?" he asked.

"No, just her sister," I said. "I think she's avoiding me." Blythe had been uncharacteristically nice to me while her sister's spell had altered her personality, and judging by her horror when the spell wore off, she'd probably be hiding underground in total mortification for the foreseeable future.

"I'm on the night shift," Nathan said. "Madame Grey

wants me to train the new security team to survive all weathers and there's meant to be a thunderstorm tonight."

"Fun." I thought of my warm, cosy house with some guilt. "We'll have to pick a day you're not on the night shift for our next date. Unless that's just wishful thinking."

He gave me a smile. "It'll get easier once some of the others pick up the slack. We're making up for years of Steve's people being lazy and taking too many shortcuts."

"As long as it keeps the hunters away," I said. "When are they coming to see Madame Grey?"

"Whenever's convenient. Is she helping with your magic lessons? I'd like to think you're getting some compensation for working at twice the pace on your interviews for her."

"She's busy," I said. "Anyway, I did learn I'm immune to Rebecca's powers and not Blythe's today."

"Really?" He paused. "Maybe it's a talent that will strengthen in time. Rebecca's a child, while Blythe is your age."

"Hmm. You don't think I'm a freak? I find something new about me every day."

"That's more common than you think, Blair, especially here." He walked me to my front door. "I have to go, but I'll be in touch after my shift's over."

"Want me to cast a waterproofing spell on you to make it easier?"

He grinned. "That's cheating. Besides, it won't be too bad. You did a great job picking out people who aren't going to drive me out of my mind."

"Always a good thing." I spotted a light in the upstairs window of the house. "Nina's in. She told me the leader of the Nightshade Coven—her old coven—used to be married to the man who died in our office."

He frowned. "Are you sure?"

"That's what Nina told me." I shrugged. "Just… seems odd that Madame Grey wouldn't mention it."

"If Madame Grey hasn't mentioned it, then she likely thinks it's not relevant to the investigation." He paused. Ah. He probably wanted to kiss me, and here I was talking about murder suspects.

"I'm used to it by now," he said.

Oops. "Did I say that out loud?"

He leaned closer and kissed me. "It's one of your endearing traits, Blair. You speak your mind."

"Meaning I have no filter." I grinned, absurdly happy. "Are you sure you don't mind all the staring? It was worse than usual tonight."

"Most of us have been the odd one out at some time or other," he said. "Honestly, when you've spent a few years here, it won't matter."

"I'm stalked by a glitter-wielding pixie, have a weird cat who can turn into a monster, and run into dead bodies on a weekly basis," I said. "That not too much for you?"

"If it was, I wouldn't like you nearly as much."

He kissed me again, up until the storm broke and drenched both of us in rainwater like we'd stepped under the falls again. It was worth every moment.

5

I arrived early at work the following morning to find the place swarming with gargoyles. Callie hovered awkwardly on the side while they rampaged around, carrying armfuls of files from Veronica's office.

"What are you doing?" I asked the nearest, whose face was still painted in stripes from the printer ink last week.

"The witches did a more thorough examination of the body," said Ink Face. "We also questioned the neighbours. Seems Veronica was spotted walking to the office around the time the murder would have taken place."

"But—she'd only just got back to town," I protested. "Even if it's true, she's already told you she didn't kill him. Twice."

"Nobody else has come forward," he said. "And she's been withholding information from the police. That merits another questioning."

"Then why are you tearing the office apart?" All my organised paperwork from yesterday was strewn across the floor.

"Evidence," he growled, as two more gargoyles ambled past carrying Veronica's desk between them.

"That's unnecessary." I stepped aside to avoid being mowed down. "How do you know it was her the neighbours saw outside? It was dark."

"She arrived back in town in the early hours of Friday morning," said the gargoyle. "The murder is known to have taken place around the same time. Plainly, she found someone breaking into her office and took matters into her own hands. Since we can't prove it was self-defence, we have no choice but to close Dritch & Co's office indefinitely."

"You can't shut us down!" I said, alarmed. "There are three other people who'll be out of a job, and she's not a murderer. Let me help. I know if she's telling the truth."

"Don't tell me what we can and can't do, Blair Wilkes," he growled. "I'd advise you to do something with your time that doesn't involve implicating yourself in your employer's crimes."

"None of us was here," I said ineffectually. Being a human lie detector was no use whatsoever when it went up against a gargoyle's hard skull.

Bethan exited our office, looking despondent. A moment later, two gargoyles stormed out, Veronica handcuffed between them. Behind, Steve marched out of her office.

"You must know you're being absurd," Bethan said to him. "With no evidence my mother committed a crime, you have no right to just lock her up without a trial."

"She'll get a trial," growled Steve. "For now, we'll see if a day in a cell loosens her tongue."

"You did that to me and I turned out to be innocent," I

told him. "Same with Keith the vampire. Given your track record, you're best assuming she's innocent until further notice."

"She's not wrong," said Veronica, and Steve looked like he wanted to hit someone.

"SHE WAS SEEN NEAR THE CRIME SCENE," the chief of police bellowed at the top of his lungs. The glass trembled in the windows, and the papers strewn in the reception swept into the air as his massive wings spread wide enough to thwack Callie in the face. She dove behind the desk with a terrified expression on her face.

My blood turned to water. *Note to self: never tick off a gargoyle.* Bit late for that, Blair.

"All I'm saying is that it might not have been her the neighbour saw," I said, my voice trembling a little. "Someone might have tried to frame her."

Steve's eyes narrowed, but Bethan stepped in. "I can think of a dozen ways the thief or the killer might have pretended to be Veronica in order to get into her office without being questioned. Or just to frame her. It's the cheapest witch trick there is. A wizard died. Is it unreasonable to expect magic to be involved?"

Steve turned on Bethan with another sweep of his wings. My brain chose that moment to imagine him in a halo on top of a Christmas tree, and I had to press the back of my knuckles to my mouth to hide my grin. *Calm down, Blair.*

"You should respect my office if you don't want to join her, Miss Eldritch," he growled at Bethan.

Her face heated bright red. "You wrecked *our* office. Are you really saying our paperwork is evidence?"

"Yes," he said, picking Veronica up by the handcuffs. "I

am. Nobody is to set foot in here again until this is cleared up." He dropped Veronica, and the other two gargoyles dragged her towards the door. Both of them were ink-splattered—it looked like the printer had given as good as it got.

"You won't get a confession from me," Veronica said, obligingly following them outside. "You're fools not to look closer under your own noses."

"And just what is that supposed to mean?" Steve demanded. "You've made a mockery of me for the last time. All of you. Get out."

We had to wait for the gargoyles to squeeze through the doors first. While two of them frog-marched Veronica away, Steve blocked our path to prevent Bethan and me from following them.

"You know I can sense lies," I said to Steve. "She told the truth when she said she didn't kill—"

"And you think I should believe you?" said Steve. "You're biased. The evidence stands. Go home, Blair."

"But—" Bethan stopped. "She's right. Blair wouldn't let a murderer walk free. She handed Mrs Dailey over just last week. At least let her sit in on the trial."

He grunted. "The trial is tomorrow. You may come and speak to us, Miss Eldritch, but if Blair is seen anywhere near the police station, she'll get a stint in a cell herself."

"You're joking," Bethan said.

"Do I look like I am?" Steve looked like if he tried to joke, he'd spontaneously combust from the pressure.

"Definitely not," I said. "Bethan—"

Ink Face blocked my path, causing me to stumble

backwards. Behind me, Lizzie and Callie stood out of reach of the gargoyle's massive wingspan.

I got the message and backed up down the road. The others did likewise, with a last sad look at Veronica's retreating figure.

Turning to the others, I said, "I'm sorry."

"This isn't your fault, Blair," said Lizzie. "If anything, it was the printer that was probably the last straw for Steve. It gave him an unwanted tattoo."

I frowned. "I didn't see any tattoos."

"You wouldn't. It was on his—"

"Are you leaving or not?" said Ink Face, who still blocked the road.

"Yep, definitely." I retreated a few steps down the street. "Did someone give Steve a quota stating that he has to arrest someone for every crime regardless of guilt, or is he just in a bad mood?"

Callie cleared her throat. "Uh, I think he heard the hunters are coming to town and got scared they'd upstage him."

"So he decided to arrest an innocent woman." I shook my head. "Sorry, guys. I... I think we should stay away from here for a bit."

"Agreed," said Lizzie. "I'm going to wait for Bethan in the café. You're welcome to come."

The idea of sitting around waiting didn't appeal. "I might join you later. There's something I need to check out first."

If I wasn't allowed to come to the police station, I wanted to do *something.* Steve's refusal to let me use my lie-sensing power to help was pure stubbornness and nothing else. Even Madame Grey had ordered me to question the security for hire despite my relative lack of qualifications, because only a mind-reader could otherwise know whether or not someone was being sincere.

If Steve refused to entertain the possibility that anyone else had committed the crime, I'd do some poking around of my own. Dr Appleton had lived and worked at the university, so the other staff would know him, if nothing else.

"Er, Blair, check out *what,* exactly?" asked Lizzie.

"Dr Appleton," I said. "The police questioned his family, right?"

"Oh," Lizzie said. "Yes, they did. I… er, also printed a spare copy of his file. Not that I'm advocating going behind Steve's back."

"He's more occupied thinking we're going to sneak back into the office," I said, taking the file she held out. "Thanks. I'll try not to annoy anyone."

"Good luck." Lizzie waved me off, and I walked to the street's end before checking the address on the file. Not the university. So he lived somewhere else when he wasn't on campus, and it was only a couple of streets away.

The sun came out as I walked, accompanied by a refreshingly cool breeze. It was a nice day to go to the lakeside, and if Alissa hadn't been at work, I might have done exactly that. If not for the lingering guilt at Veronica's arrest and the certainty that she hadn't committed a crime. Whether he felt threatened by the hunters or not, Steve was punishing an innocent person *again,* and I suspected only Madame Grey would be able to talk some sense into him.

Dr Appleton had lived in a nice house on the lakefront when he wasn't on campus. I paused outside, standing on tiptoe to see past the overgrown plants creeping over the fence. Not a gardener, apparently. A light shone behind the half-closed curtains. Someone was in. Maybe he rented out his house during term time.

A young woman with dyed pink hair answered my knock on the door. Her eyes were red-rimmed, telling me all I needed to know. "Ah, hi," I said awkwardly. "I'm— Blair Wilkes. You knew Dr Appleton?"

"He was my brother."

"Oh. I'm sorry. I—I heard this was his address, and I didn't know if anyone was living here."

"I rent from him when he's not here," she said, with a sniff. "You're not with the police, right? I already spoke to them."

"No, I work at the office where—where his body was found. I just wondered if you knew why he might have been there. The police don't seem inclined to find out."

She shook her head. "No, I haven't a clue. The Eldritch woman, the two of them used to work together ages ago, when I was a kid, but I thought they hadn't spoken in years."

"They knew one another well?" Veronica had said they were once business partners, but it didn't sound like a recent thing.

"Not for years, but that's all I know." She looked down. "I don't know what he was doing there, or who killed him."

Truth. "I heard he was married once," I said casually.

"Oh, Althea Summers. They divorced not long after," she said. "Kind of awkward considering they worked at the same university, but I guess campus is big enough they didn't run into each other much."

"She works at the university too?"

She nodded. "I thought you were a student. I've had a few people show up here asking me what happened. They all loved him."

"Sorry," I said, again. "It wasn't Veronica who killed him, but maybe I can figure out what he went to see her about. When did they work together?"

"Years ago, when he first started lecturing," she said. "Before Veronica got married and left town. He went through a phase of trying to start up his own business before he decided he preferred academic research. As far as I know, they haven't seen one another since. Unless he wanted her help with a project, but I would have thought he'd wait for her to come back first."

No lies there. And now I had a new possible lead. Dr Appleton's ex-wife might not be at the university right now, considering how close it was to the end of term, but it couldn't hurt to pay a visit to campus.

———

The gates to the town's only university campus were at the top of the hill over the northwest side of town. I passed through the gates and was swept up into a confusing maze of brick buildings painted in neon shades not unlike the printer's ink, and decorated with motifs of dragons, griffins, unicorns, and other paranormal beasts.

I stopped a passing wizard to ask which department Dr Summers worked in and was greeted with a bemused laugh. The third person I stopped told me she lectured on magical warfare, so I made my way to the north end of campus, dodging low-flying broomsticks and fox shifters playing an elaborate game with an inflatable ball with no apparent concern for passers-by. Witches and wizards practised spells on the lawns between buildings, while shifters gathered together in groups. The university seemed like a fun place to live, but I'd be at least forty before I reached junior level standards of witchcraft, at this rate, so I wouldn't be reliving my undergraduate experience anytime soon. I'd never been particularly studious, and though I'd been to a big university with a wide range of students, I'd never found a group I fit in with. That had probably been a major sign, thinking about it.

After several minutes of walking in circles and a near-collision with a pack of wizards on a flying carpet, I tracked down the right building. The inside was thankfully less confusing, with names on each door telling me who they belonged to. I paused outside Dr Summers's office, my stomach fluttering with nerves. While I'd never spoken to her, it sounded like she was pretty scary, from what Nina had said. But she didn't know me.

I knocked, and a woman maybe Rita's age answered the door Her hair was dyed black, while her face shone in such a way that suggested she'd used spells to enhance her features and smooth out wrinkles. Since her expression was almost as stern as the average gargoyle shifter, it didn't do much to make her look friendly and welcoming.

"Blair Wilkes," she said, looking down at me. She was at least a half-foot taller than I was, and skinny as a rake. "I suppose you're here to talk about my ex-husband?"

"Erm," I said, all excuses evaporating. "If you don't mind, talking, I—"

"I heard that you have a reputation for involving yourself in criminal investigations," she said. "You did the same last week, didn't you?"

"Oh," I said. "I… er, it's just that Veronica Eldritch is my boss, and she's been locked up for a murder she didn't commit. The police won't listen and she doesn't even get a trial until tomorrow, so I thought I'd find out what I can about what Dr Appleton might have been doing at her office in the meantime."

"Yes, this is at least the second time Steve has locked up someone who never committed a crime," she said. "It says volumes about our standards of policing here in Fairy Falls."

"Uh, I guess," I said. "He arrested her because someone claimed to have seen Veronica near the office when your husband died. But she's innocent. I wondered—"

"If I might have killed him?" She went on before I could speak, "My husband and I have been separated for some time, you might have heard. We've hardly seen one another in years. He spent all his time buried in the research division's library."

Truth. Besides, if she'd wanted to commit murder, Veronica's office was a weird place to have done it, considering they lived so close to one another. Unless she'd wanted to cover her tracks, but there was no need to bring Veronica into it. Right?

"Did you know Veronica?" I asked.

"Veronica Eldritch?" She gave a sniff. "No. I understand that she once entertained the idea of teaming up with my ex-husband on one of his ridiculous schemes, but he came to his senses when she left town."

"Oh." That fit with what his sister had told me. "Okay,

thanks. He worked in the research division, then. What type of research?"

"Anything that took his interest," she said. "Maybe Veronica kept some fragment of research he wanted, and he was too impatient to wait for her return before he took it for himself."

"I guess that makes sense. But he didn't die by accident, the police said. Veronica wouldn't have retaliated if she caught him in her office." I didn't *think* she would, anyway.

"I suppose you know her better than I do," she said.

True. She hadn't lied when she said she didn't know Veronica, but there was something stiff in her tone that I didn't like. Her expression told me she was closing the door in a moment whether I liked it or not. If I brought up the council, I had the feeling her façade would crack and she'd get snippy with me for being nosy. Besides, I could just ask Rita which way she'd voted. I was here to find a potential lead on a killer, not ponder the vote about the town's security system.

For the lack of anything better to do, I made my way to the department of magical research, figuring I could at least ask a few strategic questions to the people who'd known Dr Appleton professionally. Maybe they'd be able to give me more of a clue about who might have wanted to bump him off. Or at least why he'd been in Veronica's office.

The research department was located behind the library, according to the green-haired wizard I asked for directions. I made my way east, towards where a high fence divided the campus from the fields outside town, and promptly forgot all my questions when I entered the library.

I'd thought the bookshop was overwhelming, but the library was another world entirely. Dozens of towering shelves, extending to the ceiling and spreading in a labyrinthine manner. I hovered by the door, a little worried that the maze would swallow me up and I'd never get out.

A dark-skinned man with a kind face approached me. "Are you lost?"

"I'm… looking for the department of magical research."

"You're in the right place," he said. "You're not a student here, are you? No, you're…"

"Blair Wilkes," I said. "I'm a bit worried I'll get lost if I walk in there."

"You're not the first," he said. "There's signposts on all the shelves. Were you looking for a book? We're open to the public, too."

"I… not at the moment, thank you."

"Let me know if you change your mind."

"I will. Thanks." I took in a breath and dived between the rows of shelves, walking as quickly as I dared. I was kind of worried that if I ran, I'd cause a torrent of books to topple off the shelves and bury me alive. Rustling followed my steps, like the titles were whispering at my presence. I halted when the man who'd spoken to me appeared at the end of the row, making me jump. How in the world had he moved so fast?

"Left," he said. "Northwest, and keep going."

"Uhh. Thanks. How did you…?" Oh, now I saw the pointed teeth. "You're a vampire."

Considering how he'd smiled at me, I really should have spotted them sooner. And just what had my paranormal sensing power been doing, napping?

"I use an illusion spell," he said, his teeth flickering a bit. "Less alarming to the students."

"I wouldn't have thought it'd bother them," I said, taking a step back away from those flickering teeth. He'd made a better first impression than the majority of the other vampires I'd encountered, but that didn't necessarily mean anything. How had he evaded my paranormal-sensing ability? "Uh, no more than shifters or goblins, anyway."

"Or fairies?"

I took another step backwards. "Yes… are you reading my mind?"

"No, I'm not," he said. "I apologise for startling you. I wondered if that's what you were looking for in here. Information."

"What, books about fairies? Do you have any?" I hadn't exactly walked in here intending to get side-tracked, but anything that made me look less like I was nosing around a murder investigation worked in my favour. Besides, there must be thousands of books in here. Surely one of them carried a nugget of helpful information on fairies. Maybe even my own history.

"I'll take a look for you," he offered.

"Oh, thank you," I said. "I appreciate it."

The vampire disappeared swiftly, while I walked in the wrong direction for a minute before remembering he'd directed me to go left. Several diversions later, I left the maze of spiralling shelves and found a small corridor at the back under a crooked sign saying 'Research Division'.

There were three doors. One was covered in a slimy substance, and underneath was a sign saying, *Dr Appleton. Watch out for the plants: they bite.*

The door opened, and I jumped back to avoid being covered in slime. A young woman with thin wispy hair tucked into a bandana walked backwards out of Dr Appleton's office. "Yes, the unicorns will have to wait... oh, I didn't see you there." She turned around. "The professor isn't in at the moment."

"Um... he's dead." Didn't she know?

"Oh, good, they told everyone," she said distractedly. "No—not good at all. It's a disaster, actually. I'm cleaning out his office, and... are you here to help me? He left specific instructions not to touch the plants."

Given the slime on the door, I wouldn't touch anything Dr Appleton owned with a bargepole. "Er, I'm not a student. I'm—"

"Really?" she asked. "I assumed you were one of his assistants. He was always asking for volunteers to help him, like the unicorn incident, which frankly was *not* my fault..." She spoke twice as fast as anyone else I'd met, and I hadn't a hope of getting a word in edgeways, let alone taking in every word she said as she railed against Dr Appleton for his wild experiments involving undergrads.

"Er, what was he researching before he died, do you know?" I asked when she took a breath.

"Oh, everything. The magical torpedoes phase was over quickly, thankfully, and they managed to fix the roof back on..." She went off on another long tangent. And I'd thought Veronica's mind worked a mile a minute. At least his assistant was willing to talk, even if she didn't give me much chance to ask questions.

"Do you know what he might have been doing in Veronica Eldritch's office?" I squeezed in the next time she came up for air.

"Oh, no doubt to ask her an obscure question," she said, waving a hand. "He did that constantly, no matter the hour of the day—if he wanted to know something, he'd ask, whether you liked it or not."

Truth. "What project was he working on before he died?" I asked.

"He had several on the go at any given time," she said. "The man was an enigma. Eccentric, you know… constantly out in the field getting into things. Or asking for graduate students to volunteer… they stopped letting him into the academy after he swapped two students' heads. Consensually, mind, but cursing underage wizards is a good way to end up with a prison sentence."

"Oh," I said. "So he broke the law?"

"Not intentionally," she said. "He was very popular in the department and had no shortage of volunteers. If he'd applied the same level of attention to his lectures…" Her pace sped up, drowning out my every attempt to interrupt. I doubted students would be able to keep up with her in lectures either. I took a step backwards, wondering if she'd noticed if I ran, and the vampire appeared again.

"Oh, hello, Samuel," the woman said.

"Blair Wilkes," said the vampire. "I got what you were looking for."

The assistant seemed to notice the papers in her arms for the first time. "Oh, were you using the library? I won't keep you, Blair." She re-entered Dr Appleton's office, and once again, I jumped out of the way of the slime-covered door as it closed.

"Thanks for rescuing me," I said to the vampire, walking away from her office as fast as someone without a vampire's speed possibly could. "I thought she was literally going to talk my ear off."

"Being able to move swiftly does come in handy," he said, with a fanged smile. "Vera is the only person who has the patience to go through Dr Appleton's notes, so she's been in here all weekend."

"Uh, did you know Dr Appleton?" I asked. "I've learned more than I ever wanted to about his giant slug collection, but I'm lost on what project he was actually working on when he died."

"Accumulating library fines," he said, with a disapproving look over his shoulder. "He returned everything late, or damaged, or both. Anyway, I thought this might be of interest."

I took the book he offered—a volume on fairy history. "Thanks," I said gratefully.

"My pleasure. It's not every day that I meet someone with a mind as interesting as yours."

"I thought you weren't reading it."

"I caught flashes," he said, tilting his head. "You have the ability to sense the truth of a person. Interesting."

"Yeah…" *Except him.* I hadn't noticed he was a vampire at first, but then again, I *had* been overwhelmed by the labyrinth of books.

"You want to know why you couldn't sense what I was? It's part of my own ability," he said. "Believe it or not, vampires' skills can be more versatile than just reading minds."

"Really? I didn't know."

"Dr Appleton was fascinated by it," he said. "As he was

by any other paranormal novelty. He'd likely have wanted to study you, too."

"Hmm." I wasn't all that keen on the idea of being called a 'paranormal novelty', but that was beside the point. "Thanks for the book, anyway."

"Oh, keep it." He smiled with a flash of fangs. "It's not every day I meet a fairy."

"No…" I paused. "I guess you probably know I'm here because of Dr Appleton. You can read minds, so—do you know anyone here who'd have reason to have him killed?"

"One of his ex-assistants? He usually returns them in one piece." He grinned. "No, that was a joke. They loved him. He didn't die on the campus, and I think it more likely that he was caught trespassing and died through a spell used in self-defence. He did like to dive into situations before assessing the potential consequences."

But Veronica didn't do it. "Thanks anyway." I put the textbook into my bag and turned away from the towering shelves, with more questions than ever.

A vampire lecturer who could hide what he was even from my paranormal-sensing power? That was a new one. Compared to Dr Appleton, though, Samuel seemed relatively sane and normal. And as a bonus, the new book on fairies he'd given me might come in handy.

6

I promptly found myself lost again the instant I exited the research building. I hadn't realised the campus covered the entire northwest side of the town right up to the forest border, not until I took a wrong turning and found a signpost saying 'Shifter territory beyond this point. Please use the east exit. DO NOT CLIMB THE FENCE.'

There were more than a few werewolves running around the lawns—in human form, that is. The university wasn't exclusively for witches and wizards, though some types of practical magical study would only be accessible to people who could use a wand. I stopped beside the fence. Really, it'd be quicker to jump over than find my way through the maze of campus. Maybe there was a safe place to climb the fence where I wouldn't run into any werewolves. I switched on my Seven Millimetre Boots and levitated a few inches, then froze when I heard the murmur of voices from the other side of the fence. That was Madame Grey's voice. What was she doing all the way out by the town's border?

I touched down to earth and moved closer, my footsteps soft, hoping nobody had seen the top of my head poking over the fence.

Madame Grey's voice grew louder. "I told you, we have enough security guards of our own," she was saying. "It's very valiant of you to offer your skills, but they're not needed."

"That's for Inquisitor Hare to decide," said a familiar voice, belonging to a hunter I'd nicknamed Grumpy when I'd encountered him and two of his buddies in the woods. Sleepy, Dopey and Grumpy. What was he doing here?

I cast a quick spell to make myself unobtrusive, then levitated so my head rested just underneath the top of the fence. I'd look ridiculous from behind, but nobody on campus seemed to want to get this close to the border.

"No, it's for me to decide who enters this town," said Madame Grey, loudly and clearly. "If Inquisitor Hare wishes to speak to me, he can do so in person, not by sending his underlings. Of course, if it turns out that we don't need your help, then there'll be no need to stay. The people who are selected to work for us would naturally have to pass our stringent interview process."

Ha. I guess the three idiots hadn't made the best of impressions. Not that that was anything new. Why would they even be allowed back into the town after they'd been kicked out for trespassing?

"The Inquisitor thinks the town needs a thorough inspection," said Sleepy.

"Not hardly," said Madame Grey. "The unfortunate incident which prompted Fairy Falls to be added to the hunters' list is over and we're in the process of training a talented new security team. In the meantime, I find it interesting that you three came here unaccompanied when your descriptions match those on the police report from a trespassing incident. We have no need for outside help, least of all from you."

Go, Madame Grey! She was up to speed on Mrs Dailey's antics at the border last week. Not that it made the three hunters' presence here any less worrying.

"Inquisitor Hare cleared us of all wrongdoing," said Sleepy. "And we heard you're still looking for security guards."

"We're not currently open for applications," she said. "If we are in future, I'll be sure to call the Inquisitor myself." *Lie.* Not that I blamed her. Even if those three weren't Mrs Dailey's former helpers, there was no way to run interviews without giving away that the owner of the town's sole recruitment firm was in jail on suspicion of murder. A sudden surge of guilt rose within me, for failing to learn anything new about why Dr Appleton might have broken into Veronica's office. What did she have that he couldn't have found in that giant library?

A louder voice rose from behind the fence, and I jumped, nearly exposing my head. "You should never have let them pass," said Chief Donovan of the werewolf pack. "We don't want hunters here."

"They never crossed the border," said Madame Grey. "They asked to speak to me specifically."

"They are making a mockery of us by coming this close to our territory," said the werewolf in a low voice. "If they get any closer—"

"Don't worry," she said. "If Inquisitor Hare does indeed pay a visit, you'll get adequate warning first."

"Not good enough," said the werewolf chief. "I'll have to tell my pack to prepare, naturally."

"Do that," said Madame Grey. "The incident at Callie's office last week was in no way her fault, but we can't afford to have any more mishaps."

"I know that better than you do," growled Chief Donovan. "They're my people. I will not have a single pack member harmed by those hunters. If they move to this town, we're leaving, and we'll never come back."

"That won't be necessary," she said. "I have no intention of allowing the hunters to make a permanent base here. No, I suspect that the person who seeks to unseat me had a hand in this."

So it's true. Someone wants to replace the town's leader. But did she mean Blythe's mother, or someone else?

"That's your business, not mine," said Chief Donovan. "See to it that none of my people is harmed while you sort out your feud."

I waited for him to leave, then levitated to the top of the fence. Checking he'd disappeared into the trees, I used my boots to hop over the fence and join Madame Grey. She turned on the spot, drawing her wand.

"Goddess, Blair, are you trying to startle me to death?" Her wand lowered, gleaming with silvery light.

"Sorry," I said. "I got lost on the campus and I couldn't help overhearing you and those hunters."

"Blair, usually, you *can* help what you overhear. However, given your involvement with those particular hunters, I suppose I can't fault you for curiosity."

"It's not just curiosity," I said. "I was concerned. Who's Inquisitor Hare?"

"The leader of the region's largest hunter branch," she said. "It seems I have to prepare for a visit."

My heart dropped. "But—Veronica's in jail. Do they know?"

"Certainly not," she said. "If the subject of Dritch & Co comes up, I'll handle it, but since I interview all the possible security guards myself, they won't need to ask for more details. You sent some good people, Blair, and they'll start working with Nathan immediately."

"Oh. That's good." But would it be enough for the hunters? "Veronica's trial is tomorrow. Have you spoken to Steve?"

"Not today. I was diverted by reports of hunters at the borders again." She flashed a disgruntled look over her shoulder. "Steve will be even less happy if I tell him how close they got."

"I was told the reason he flipped out and locked up Veronica was because he wanted to compensate for being completely ineffective. Uh, not that I'd tell the hunters that."

"I would prefer to avoid mentioning it," she said. "If the hunters deem our law enforcement ineffective, they have permission to take over, which is the last thing any of us needs."

"Since when did the word of Sleepy, Dopey and Grumpy take precedence over the person who actually runs the town?"

"The word of *who?*"

"I gave them nicknames. Since I don't know their real names."

"I see," she said. "The hunters… like them, we're doing our best to deal with a lot of magically gifted people living in a small space while trying not to draw the normals' attention. We share a common goal with the hunters—to live peacefully and to protect humanity."

Some of them, maybe. But while those three might have claimed to have been pardoned, I'd bet they weren't here for the good of humanity, let alone peace. They were in it for their own gain, pure and simple.

"Doesn't sound like Steve," I commented. "How'd he end up running the police in the first place?"

"Nobody else wanted the job," she said simply. "It's one thing to run a coven, it's another to police a diverse range of citizens without favouring one group over the others. The gargoyles are impartial observers who can judge situations without letting personal grudges get in the way. We've had much fewer disruptions under the gargoyles than other magical towns who've let the vampires or the shifters police all citizens. Or even the witches."

"They're not impartial," I pointed out. "They prioritised the werewolves over the vampires when they nearly went to war. And now they've locked Veronica up when they know perfectly well that anyone might have pretended to be her using a simple illusion spell."

"Precisely why I involve myself in any cases where it's clear that there has been magical interference," she said. "However, Steve has the final verdict. It's that way for a reason. If a powerful magical leader turned to corruption and they were also in charge of the law enforcement, the results would be dire for everyone. It's happened before, in other towns."

Corruption? "You think someone's trying to unseat you, don't you?"

"It's no big secret, Blair," she said. "Half the coven leaders would like to be in my place."

"Blythe's mother," I said. "She's the one who knocked out the guards and let the hunters in. And she nearly succeeded in convincing the council to replace you while you were gone. Might she have told the hunters to come back and try again before she was jailed?"

"What Mrs Dailey did is only a culmination of many issues that've been growing in Fairy Falls for months," she said. "We'll get through this rough spot."

I found it hard to share her faith. If the hunters found out Steve had a track record of being inept, they'd have the authority to step in and take over. As irritating as the gargoyle shifter was, taking orders from Sleepy, Dopey and Grumpy was hardly better.

"I really think Steve should have let Veronica go," I said. "In the human world, usually it's innocent until proven guilty, not the other way around. That's what they say, anyway. Steve just seems to toss the nearest available target in jail rather than face admitting he doesn't know who did it."

"What justification did he use?" she asked. "The other gargoyles wouldn't have acted without one."

"Well, a neighbour thought she saw Veronica on the way to the office around the time Dr Appleton was supposed to have died," I admitted. "But it might have been someone else using an illusion spell or potion. I mean, Blythe's little sister used an illusion spell to pretend to be Blythe when she went to visit the office the other weekend. Even she could cast a spell that simple."

Her lips pursed. "Veronica will have a chance to defend herself at her trial tomorrow, and I'll be there, Blair. I'll do my best to help."

"Thanks," I said. "Because Steve won't take my word alone."

Madame Grey scanned my face. "Blair, I know it must be doubly frustrating for you, with you able to sense lies the way you can. I never pushed for the police to hire witches as lie detectors, for reasons I'm sure you'll be able to guess."

I frowned. Then it hit me. "Blythe's family? They're the only people with the ability, right? Except my mum, but she—she left."

The idea of Mrs Dailey being in charge of verifying whether or not someone was being truthful gave me chills. If her coven had run the town and the law enforcement, it wouldn't have been a pleasant place to live at all.

"Precisely. It's not a common talent at all," Madame Grey said. "As for the vampires, we've never been able to persuade any of them to use their talents to help the police. There's no law dictating that we *have* to use all our magical abilities, after all."

"Oh, of course," I said. "But I know Veronica is innocent. Unless Steve thinks *I'm* a liar, but any vampire can verify that I'm not."

Her mouth pressed together in a line. "Unless you're able to get hold of a vampire willing to help you out by tomorrow, that's unlikely to hold up, Blair."

Samuel? No, I barely knew the guy. Vincent was the only vampire I was on speaking terms with, unless you counted Alissa's ex, Keith, but he hadn't reached the mind-reading stage the last I'd heard. Also, he'd spent time in jail himself for a crime he'd never committed, and I was pretty sure he didn't want to repeat the performance if he ticked off Steve.

That left me one option… find the real culprit. Or at least an ironclad reason why Veronica couldn't have committed the murder. If the killer had pretended to be her, long enough to fool the neighbours who happened to have been looking out the window, that didn't leave me with a lot of options. I'd really hoped I'd find more clues in Dr Appleton's department on campus, but I was still thoroughly in the dark.

Maybe I should try talking to Vincent. Okay, he'd let me down on more than one occasion. Including just last week. Unless I bribed him, but what could I possibly use to bribe a seven-hundred-year-old billionaire vampire? I might as well teach my cat to juggle.

On the other hand, he had come through for me against Blythe's mother in the end. It was worth a try.

———

Five minutes later, against my better judgement, I knocked on the front door of the vampires' headquarters. It stood adjacent to the cemetery, next to the local funeral home. I'd heard vampires ran the place since they made the best coffin-makers. Dr Appleton's body would be kept there until his funeral. Meanwhile, his killer walked free.

Guilt twisted inside me. I'd been preoccupied trying to prove my boss's innocence, but while she remained incarcerated, the actual killer walked among us, maybe in plain sight.

The door opened after my second knock, but it wasn't

Vincent who answered. Instead, Lord Anderson stood on the doorstep. He looked older than most vampires I'd seen, with greying hair and wrinkles, but still several hundred years younger than his actual age.

"Yes, Blair?" he said. "What is it?"

"Oh, hey, Lord Anderson," I said. "I'm looking for Vincent. I need a mind-reader."

"Oh?" He raised an eyebrow.

"My boss is in jail for a murder she didn't commit," I explained. "I already used my lie-sensing ability to tell the police she didn't do it, but they won't take my word for it. So I thought they might if a vampire backed up what I said."

"An interesting thought," he said. "Unfortunately, we're forbidden to use our gifts to interfere with police investigations."

"What? But she's innocent. You only need to dive into my thoughts to see it."

"No, Blair, I do not."

"I..." I blinked. "Can't you read my thoughts? Or..."

I'm blocking him. I did it to Samuel, too.

"The police wouldn't take the word of someone like me, besides," Lord Anderson said. "Given my prior convictions."

"Oh, because you bit Keith," I said, my heart sinking. "But it's not like we ever really spoke outside of that investigation. You're impartial."

"I think you know that the gargoyle police chief seems determined to believe the worst of you... and everyone else."

I groaned. "If you could read my thoughts, you'd know it's the worst possible time for the owner of Dritch & Co to be jailed. It would help if the police just *employed* a reliable mind-reader."

"Reading minds is not fool-proof," said Lord Anderson. "Vampires lie and deceive one another all the time. Would you want them deciding the fates of others?"

Ah. Good point. And he would know, since nobody had figured out he'd bitten Keith until he'd confessed to it.

"And apparently some of us can block one another," I added. "Is there no other way to get Veronica off the hook, short of catching the culprit?"

"I thought you were adept at this by now, Blair," he said.

I shook my head. "Anyone could have killed the guy. The police don't seem to be chasing leads at all. Are you sure Vincent's not around?"

"I'll let him know you wanted to see him, Blair."

That was the best I'd get. "Okay. I don't suppose you know how I blocked you, exactly? I didn't even know I was doing it."

Lord Anderson paused for a long moment. "Usually, it's affected by skill level," he said. "Maybe in your case, there's another factor. I will speak to Vincent."

He closed the door before I could say another word. *That was abrupt.*

Usually it's affected by skill level... oh. He meant *my* skill level must be stronger than his in order for me to block him, unless there was another reason. Vampire egos were delicate, apparently.

Assuming it was true, could I only be read by the most powerful mind-readers? That made Blythe more powerful than she let on. Pity she wasn't still under Rebecca's spell, but Blythe would happily see Veronica jailed for life. And now Madame Grey had put the mental image of Mrs Dailey running the jail in my head, I'd been thoroughly put off involving *any* mind-readers in the investigation. No, I had to trust Madame Grey would do everything she could to get Veronica off the hook. In the meantime, I'd do my best to piece together what had happened to Dr Appleton. He'd seemed an inconsistent individual from what I'd heard even without taking his sudden death into account. But I didn't believe for a minute he'd been in Veronica's office by coincidence alone.

When I got home, Nina was on her way out. "Hey, Blair," she said. "I thought you were at work."

"I was, until my boss got arrested again."

"Oh, no." Her mouth turned down at the corners. "Do the police think she really did it?"

"She didn't," I said. "But try telling Steve anything he doesn't want to hear. Her trial's tomorrow, so I'm off until then." I stepped aside to let Nina pass, but I couldn't help remembering she'd once been part of the Nightshade Coven. Like Dr Summers. "Uh, I wondered—was Dr Appleton ever a member of the Nightshade Coven?"

"You spoke to his ex-wife?" she guessed. "Yes, he was a member in theory, but in all honesty, he never did much for the coven. He was always busy with work instead."

"Yeah, it sounds like he was dedicated to his research," I said. "I spoke to Dr Summers in person. She seems... intense." She'd also anticipated my questions, but she definitely hadn't lied when she said she hadn't killed him.

"She has a strong personality. It's why she and my mother clashed."

"Did Dr Summers support the hunters?" I said.

"I honestly don't know," said Nina. "She wouldn't have wanted them to come into the town, I don't think. I hope they don't end up sticking around."

"Me neither."

Would Dr Summers have had reason to frame Veronica for her ex-husband's death? If she wanted the hunters here, taking Dritch & Co out of the picture definitely made their job easier. But half the council had voted in favour of bringing in external security. That didn't make them bad people—just look at Nathan. It was more the timing of Veronica's arrest that bothered me. Not to mention Steve's pig-headed stubbornness.

I said goodbye to Nina and made my way into the flat. There, I found Alissa half-lying on the sofa with Roald sprawled on top of her.

"Hey," she said, stroking Roald on the head. "I heard about your boss. Where've you been all morning?"

I dumped my bag, which made a clunking noise as the fairy textbook Samuel had given me fell over. "I went poking around the university where Dr Appleton worked."

She rolled her eyes. "Of course you did. What did you find out?"

I ran through my misadventures on campus, and my disturbing encounter with the hunters at the border.

"Whoa," she said. "They're really overstepping their boundaries. I wonder if they even called Madame Grey before they showed up or if she just happened to walk that way because she thought they'd try something."

"Either," I said. "They were the same hunters who trespassed before and got kicked out. And worked with Blythe's mother. Supposedly they got acquitted, but you'd think the hunters would keep tabs on these things."

Alissa shifted into a sitting position. "What did my grandmother do?"

"It sounds like she's going to have to speak to their boss in person to tell them flat-out that there's no need for them to come to town," I said. "It seems he's dead set on coming here to check our security's adequate. Not really helpful when Veronica's in jail. I can't help thinking the person behind this was counting on her being out of the picture."

Her eyes widened. "What, you think someone killed that guy to frame her?"

"I don't know what to believe," I admitted. "It just seems random that he'd show up dead in her office. There's no connection there."

"Someone planted his body there to frame her," Alissa guessed. "Someone who'd have something to gain from his murder."

"Dr Summers," I said. "But she *said* she didn't do it and my lie detector didn't go off. I should have asked what *her* magical gift was."

"Oh, she's gifted at elemental magic," she said. "I know most of the council members' gifts and so does Madame Grey. She's definitely no mind-reader."

"Hmm." I frowned. "I don't think it was a coincidence that the husband of a council member who's probably pro-hunter was the person who died, in the office of someone who was supposed to be interviewing the town's new security members."

"Yeah, that's way too fishy to be a coincidence," she said. "If they found no clues at the crime scene, the body *might* have been planted there."

"I don't know about clues at the crime scene," I said. "Steve and the gargoyles seemed more intent on making a mess of Veronica's paperwork than anything else. I wish they'd let me sit in on the trial, but I can't make an open accusation against a council member with zero proof. Not to mention she thinks the police are inadequate herself, and so do the hunters."

Alissa grimaced. "Oh. Yeah, that's a good point."

"The only other person I know is up to no good is Mrs Dailey," I said. "And unless she's talking to people from behind bars, making that accusation won't work in my favour either."

"I don't think it's possible for anyone to get into the high-security area of the prison," Alissa said. "Not that I have personal experience. I'd say it's more likely that Mrs Dailey set up her scheme before she was jailed at all."

"And Dr Summers is carrying on with her legacy?" I suggested. "Well, my cat broke into the jail once. And the pixie can even get into the LFPF, which is supposed to be impenetrable."

"I'd wait for the trial to be over before you do anything rash, Blair," said Alissa. "For all we know, Steve might be in a generous mood tomorrow."

"And if not? Veronica will be stuck in jail as long as the average murder sentence is here. Probably longer than Blythe's mother, since she was jailed for conspiring against Madame Grey, not murder."

She winced. "As you said, there's no proof. Did my

grandmother say who the hunters were sending to inspect the town?"

"Someone called Inquisitor Hare, whoever he is."

Her eyes rounded. "Blair, he's the owner of the LFPF."

My heart tried to jump out of my chest. "You mean—he owns the place my dad's locked up in?"

"Yes, and more," she said. "If he's carrying out the inspection in person… no. I wouldn't have thought they'd go that far. Not for a first inspection."

"Madame Grey seemed set on speaking to him," I said. "As long as he doesn't come near Veronica's trial. It's bound to go badly. Either she gets locked up for life or word gets out that the police are in the habit of frequently jailing innocent people if they can't find anyone else. Is this Inquisitor person really that bad?"

"My grandmother will handle him." Her knuckles whitened as her fists clenched. "But yes, he does have a reputation. More than the hunters, if possible. He's the man behind their whole operation."

I rubbed my forehead, suddenly tired beyond measure. "Wonderful. *How* Sleepy, Dopey and Grumpy ended up reporting to him… I suppose that's why they got off the hook for helping Mrs Dailey."

"Probably." Alissa got up off the sofa, her feet catching on my bag. It lay where I'd dropped it, the textbook halfway out. "What's the book for?"

"Oh, I forgot about that." I picked it up. "Got it from the university campus library. It's a book on fairy history."

"Neat," said Alissa, reading the title over my shoulder. "I did wonder if there was a fairy equivalent to our witch textbooks."

"Rita mentioned at my magic lesson that my fairy

magic can't be tested like witchcraft because there's no curriculum for it." I settled the textbook in my lap. "All I know I can do is glamour and un-glamour. Maybe that's what I should have asked my dad about."

"Go for it," she said. "Has he responded to your last letter?"

"No. I tried asking if anyone else in my family is alive, like you said, but he hasn't sent a reply. I guess it's too risky for him to write that in a letter. Next time I'll ask him about my magic."

Maybe dad could tell me if my ability to block mind-reading powers came from his side of the family or not. And if it was possible to control it. I flipped the textbook open, while Alissa picked up the *Guide to Fairies and Other Species* I'd left on the coffee table.

"This one says a little about magic," she commented. "Have you read it?"

"Possibly." I closed the new textbook and leaned over to look at the page she'd opened. "I skimmed it. Didn't really tell me anything specific to fairies and not pixies."

"Well, there's a section here on glamour," she said. "It says it means changing how others perceive you rather than your actual appearance. If you wanted to, you could make yourself look like another person using the same magic. Like an illusion spell."

"Huh." I scanned the page. "Oh. I didn't know... that's how the pixie turns invisible. That's a glamour, too."

Which meant I might be able to do the same.

"Blair, your last attempt at invisibility didn't exactly end well for anyone involved."

She wasn't wrong. "No, I just... That must be how the pixie's able to sneak in and out of jail to visit my dad."

If I could turn invisible, maybe I could sneak into the town jail and question Blythe's mother on whether or not she was responsible for framing Veronica. Or maybe I was best off leaving that to the pixie. Veronica's trial was tomorrow, after all.

———

The following morning, I woke to a message from Madame Grey conditionally inviting me to Veronica's trial. Since I'd planned to come and try to persuade Steve to let me in anyway, I'd had an early night after spending the evening trying to create a new glamour. All I'd managed to do was scare off the cats, so I'd written another note to my dad to give to the pixie next time it showed up asking for some advice about glamouring. I'd also read some of the textbook on fairy history, but to my disappointment, I'd quickly discovered that it was filled with more speculation than fact. After all, it was written by a human, and the fairies were stingy with sharing their secrets.

For now, all I could do was show up for Veronica's trial. Madame Grey would be there, and Bethan, so I didn't feel totally alone. The latter met me outside the police station.

"Hey, Blair," Bethan said. She was dressed up in smart clothes and looked distinctly uncomfortable. "Did Madame Grey let you come?"

"Conditionally." The 'condition' probably being that I kept my mouth shut.

Clare, the receptionist, nodded at us. She was huge and stocky and disliked me about one percent less than the other gargoyles, which wasn't saying much, but she didn't raise any objections to my presence here.

"None of the vampires volunteered to help?" asked Bethan quietly.

"Alissa told you?" I guessed. "It was a long shot. And they're not really trustworthy either. I just hoped Madame Grey would talk some sense into Steve."

"Speak of the devil," Bethan whispered.

Madame Grey swept in, shepherding Bethan and me along with her until we reached the main trial room. Unlike the interrogation rooms, it was wide and large and seemed designed to fit exactly ten gargoyles along the back wall, wing-to-wing. Seats circled one larger central chair more like a throne, which was covered in metal chains. My chest tightened. I hadn't thought they'd use the trial room usually reserved for dangerous serial killers.

Steve glowered at me as he walked in, but he didn't stop me taking a seat next to Bethan. More gargoyles followed, and then Ink Face came in with Veronica in handcuffs. He deposited her in the big throne-like chair, where the chains immediately folded themselves over her body, pinning her in place. My stomach lurched. She hadn't even been found guilty yet, and it wasn't like she was capable of attacking anyone without a wand. Bethan's face went chalk white.

"Madame Grey." Steve nodded to the leading witch as she took a seat directly in front of Veronica's chair. "Good. Everyone's here. Veronica Eldritch, explain what you were doing when Dr Appleton's body was discovered."

I held my tongue while Veronica answered the same questions over and over again. Her visible impatience was understandable considering how many interrogations she'd already been through.

"You claim not to have spoken to Dr Appleton in years, correct?" Steve asked her.

"No," she said. "We spoke just that morning."

All eyes turned to her. *Huh? She didn't mention that before.*

"You spoke the morning he died?" Steve's eager expression made me want to throw up.

"Yes, I caught him outside my office," Veronica said. "I then went home to drop off my possessions before returning to the office after an hour or so. I assumed he'd left before my employees showed up for work, but I returned to my office to find his body lying in the doorway."

"You didn't mention that in either of our last two interrogations," said Steve.

No… she hadn't. But my lie-detector was silent. She told the truth.

"I suppose I didn't." Veronica shifted upright in the chained seat, her expression oddly calm despite her dire predicament.

"So you found him at the office, and then you killed him?" Steve asked.

"No," she said. "I didn't kill him."

No lies. But why would she wait until now to mention they'd talked that morning? I would have thought she'd have bought that up at the first questioning, just to avoid any unwelcome surprises later.

"Then why did you go to the office twice?" he said, his wings bristling.

"I told you," Veronica said. "I arrived back in town and

ran into Dr Appleton outside my office. I needed to pick up some things from my house, so I left and came back later."

"What did you discuss when you met him?"

"Nothing of your concern."

I winced. So did Bethan.

"She was under a spell," Bethan put in. "The curse. It altered her personality."

Steve whirled on her. "Did it make her kill him?"

"She already said she didn't," I interjected. "And she didn't lie."

"She omitted pertinent information," said Steve.

Even Madame Grey couldn't argue with that. I looked desperately at Veronica, but her gaze was on the door.

"This is inconclusive," Madame Grey said. "There's no advice I can offer at this stage other than to question anyone else who might have had reason to murder Dr Appleton."

"That won't be necessary." Steve's voice was flat. "Veronica Eldritch has given us all the information we need. Please return her to her cell."

And that was that. The chains on the chair released Veronica to the gargoyles once again, and her blank expression was the last thing I saw before the doors closed on her.

Bethan rose to her feet. "Please—"

"Get out," Steve said. "Blair Wilkes—"

"Enough," said Madame Grey. "You may have the authority to jail my fellow witches, but not to speak to them in such a disrespectful manner. Blair, Bethan, I'd advise you to leave."

Even Madame Grey couldn't salvage the situation. We were screwed.

Bethan was silent as we walked out, and I saw tears glinting in her eyes, probably more from frustration than anything. "I'm sorry," I said to her.

"Me, too."

Sandwiched between two gargoyles, Veronica moved at a leisurely pace, too calm for someone potentially facing a life sentence. What was wrong with her? She might not be the type to panic, but the uncharacteristic calm… something wasn't right.

It wasn't until I'd left the police station far behind that it finally hit me. I'd seen that blank look in her eyes somewhere before.

I'd seen it on Blythe… when she'd been under mind control.

8

"Mind control?" Alissa said later, when she'd returned from her shift to find me pacing the living room. "Are you sure?"

"Positive." I paced around the sofa, making Sky give me a disgruntled look for disturbing his nap. "I've seen that look before. And the person who did it is in jail right now."

"The guy who killed Mr Bayer?"

"Simeon Clarke." I shivered, rubbing my goosebump-covered arms. "He got an innocent man to commit murder once before. Maybe *he's* behind this, not Mrs Dailey."

I'd wondered if Dr Appleton had ended up near Veronica's office because someone had moved his body there after killing him. Mind control added a whole other dimension of possibilities. When I'd first moved here, Simeon Clarke had bewitched another wizard into poisoning someone so he could get around my lie-sensing powers without my knowing he was behind the murder.

"I'm not sure he can use his powers from the jail," said Alissa. "He shouldn't be able to, anyway."

"The police aren't at their most observant right now," I said. "Certain gargoyles aren't, anyway. I've never seen anything other than mind control have that effect on someone."

"Are you absolutely sure? The mind control's not a permanent thing, right?"

I shook my head. "I don't think so. It's been a while, but I think it requires eye contact and needs to be used constantly or the person will just go back to normal. But it lets him erase memories, too. He was seriously scary. If I hadn't had my own mind powers, I don't know what he'd have done to me."

She sucked in a breath. "If the police didn't see it, you'd have a hell of a job proving she was under mind control. Especially if she didn't remember."

"You might know it." I rested my hands on the back of the sofa, thinking hard. If Veronica had been hit by mind control, who else in the jail might have experienced the same? Worse, she was going back into prison with the person who'd done it. And with Mrs Dailey. She'd have recognised another person gifted in mind magic right off. Even prison bars didn't block her from reading minds. I'd bet my wand she'd recruited him there and then.

But there was no way to prove it. They'd never believe me.

I have to do something. I paced around the sofa once again and spotted the open textbook. Fairy magic. Glamour... "If I mastered invisibility, I could sneak in."

"Uh, Blair, you know what happened last time you made an invisibility potion," said Alissa.

"Hey, I only got one part wrong. Anyway, what's the alternative? The hunters are coming. If they get into the jail and find someone putting mind-control spells on people from behind bars..."

Alissa paled. "Okay, you have a point there. But there are so many things that could go wrong with breaking into the jail. Like getting jailed yourself."

"I know," I said. "But the alternative is to do nothing, and—it fits. Simeon is the exact sort of person Mrs Dailey would want working for her. I know they're both in jail, but there's no way to know for certain unless I go in there and look myself."

"All right." Alissa pulled out her wand. "Let's see you try the glamour."

———

Several hours of failed invisibility later, Alissa took to the kitchen with her potion-making equipment, having procured a stash of ingredients from Madame Grey's stores to have a real go at making an invisibility potion that didn't turn into a transparency one. I trusted her more with the potion than myself, so I stuck with practising my fairy magic. Not that I was having much luck. Shifting between human and fairy modes became easier by the minute, but that seemed to be all I could do.

Sky woke up from his nap when I was hovering in the air waving my arms around, looking up at me with his best judgemental expression.

"Yes, I know I look like a fool," I told him. "I don't suppose you can teach me how to turn invisible?"

He yawned widely, showing all his teeth, and curled up on the sofa again.

I fluttered back down to pet him, rereading the textbook as I did so. According to the book, fairies usually controlled their human glamour rather than having someone else put the glamour on. From what I could work out, the glamour I'd worn most of my life had been set to age along with me. If I learned how to control the glamour myself, I'd be able to change my appearance however I liked. Unfortunately, the person who'd written the book seemed as in the dark as me as to how to *control* that power. Only my dad could help me with that.

I put the book down and stood with my right hand palm-up, feeling for the spark that appeared whenever I switched my glamour. It came and went inconsistently. I flapped my right hand in the air, hoping to catch it. Sky looked away as though ashamed to be in the same room as me.

"Blair, you look like you're swatting a fly," Alissa said, glancing up from the potion boiling on the stove.

"Pretty sure it's how I de-glamoured at least once. I don't know, it's not like fairies have wands. Sky, give me a hand here?"

"Miaow." He closed his eyes. Nice to have a supportive familiar.

I beat my wings, hovering up and down in mid-air. At least I was getting better at flying, but that wouldn't help me to break into the jail to interrogate Simeon. Or Mrs Dailey. The very idea of talking to either of them again, even behind bars, was terrifying. And if they refused to confess, I'd have no proof. Nobody had seen that look in

Veronica's eyes, the hint of mind control, except me. Not even Madame Grey.

Alissa stirred the potion, while I turned on the spot, waving my right hand. "Vanish, vanish, vanish."

"Uh, Blair, maybe you shouldn't do that," she said. "What if you can't turn visible again?"

"If in doubt, do the same thing again until it works. The book doesn't give me any clues." Annoyance gripped me. The pixie wasn't around, and Sky wouldn't help me a bit even though I knew full well he could use the same glamour if he wanted to. "Vanish, *vanish*—"

Sky disappeared.

"Uh. Did you mean to do that, Sky?" I stared at the spot where the cat had disappeared. "Sky, come back."

"MIAOW," he yowled irritably.

Oh no. I'd turned the *cat* invisible. And… "Roald?" I asked.

A second pitiful mewl came from beside him.

Alissa whirled around, leaving the boiling potion. "Where's Roald?"

Uh-oh. "I don't know. I mean, I was thinking about the cats, but I was more annoyed at the textbook."

"MIAOW," said Sky.

A quieter meow came from his side. Alissa's eyebrows disappeared into her hairline. "Blair…"

"I'm sorry. I don't know how it happened."

Her forehead scrunched up. "I'm going to finish this potion before it sets on fire. Blair, please tell me you know how to undo it."

I waved my right hand frantically. "Ah. There's got to be a magical equivalent to a delete button."

"If you delete my familiar, Blair, I'll vanish *you*," said

Alissa irritably, her hair standing on end from the potion fumes. "Sorry. I'm not mad at you, but seriously, can you undo it?"

"I'm trying." I waved my hand around, not sure *how* I'd done it to begin with. Sky set up a yowl that Roald echoed with enthusiasm, and I sank into an armchair, my head pounding. "Guys, I can't concentrate with you doing that."

Sky did an alarmingly accurate impression of a werewolf.

Alissa moved the potion off the stove. "It's done. It has to be drunk or used within an hour otherwise it'll go off."

"And it only lasts two hours," I said, glancing at the clock. "I'll have to undo the glamour on the cats when I get back. If they stop yowling at me."

"MIAOW," Sky bellowed in my ear.

Alissa winced. "We won't get any sleep if you don't."

"Sky," I said. "I'm going to need you to help with—"

"MIAOW."

Alissa shook her head. "Somehow, I don't think he'll come and help you create a diversion."

I groaned. "What's the alternative?"

She pursed her lips. "I can take the potion, too. But Blair, you're best at accidental diversions."

"What, like glitter balls? They'd know it's me."

"Good point." She dug a spoon into the potion and began doling it out between two mugs. "You owe me for this."

"I'll do all your grocery shopping for a month."

"Done." She spooned the potion into the mugs. "If my grandmother finds out, she'll skin both of us alive."

"We're doing this for her sake as well as Veronica's," I said.

Alissa handed me the mug. "That's the only reason I'm going ahead with this scheme, Blair. If the hunters are coming for the gargoyles, they won't stop until they unseat Madame Grey. I won't let them do it."

She downed the contents of the mug and vanished. I drank down my own portion, grimacing at the bitter taste, and my body faded from view.

"Nice job," I said.

"Didn't forget the nettles," she said. "In fairness, transparency is probably the least harmful thing that could have gone wrong last time."

"You're right." I looked for the direction of her voice and yelped when an invisible claw dug into me. "Ow. Sky, how do you know where I—"

"MIAOW."

"I promise I'll fix you as soon as we get back." I backed away from the sofa and tripped over a solid invisible body. "Sky, if I break my neck, I won't be able to undo the spell. I'll be back in less than two hours."

"Blair, you might want to stick close to me while we walk, so neither of us goes missing," said Alissa.

"Good idea." I checked my wand was securely in my pocket, as were my keys and phone. Everything I already had on me was invisible, but I wouldn't be able to pick up anything new without it floating there giving the game away.

Sky let out a horrible yowl as I approached the door.

"I'll be back soon," I said to the empty flat. "Promise."

Alissa and I crept outside, leaving the sound of howling cats behind. It didn't seem like a good omen. Neither did the full moon. I wore my levitating boots rather than going in fairy-mode, because leaving a trail of glitter all over the jail was a dead giveaway. I kept losing track of Alissa in the dark, and she gripped onto the back of my coat to stay behind me.

"This is awkward," she muttered. "I can see through you, but not, and… ow. You kicked me in the shin."

"Sorry," I said, floating more lopsidedly than usual with her hanging onto me. "I had enough trouble being transparent, never mind this. We're almost there."

I slowed my pace as we neared the jail, and paused out of earshot of the massive gargoyle standing on guard outside.

"I could send up a glitter ball to get him to move, but they probably know it's my signature move by now," I whispered.

"I'll handle it. You stay out of sight until the guard moves." She let go of my coat and vanished into the dark.

I drew in a deep breath and held still until there was a flash of light at the end of the road, followed by a very convincing howl.

Oh. The full moon. Good thinking, Alissa.

The gargoyle outside the entrance to the jail shifted, frowning into the dark. "Bloody werewolves."

The howling grew louder. Either Alissa was using an amplifying spell or she had some hitherto-unknown skill at making wolf noises. The gargoyle marched forwards. "Get back into the woods. Idiot drunks."

"AWOOOOOO!" Alissa called.

The gargoyle yanked the jail door open. "There's a drunken wolf making trouble again."

The door opened and another gargoyle barged out into the night. "Cut that out, wolf, you hear me!"

For a moment, the door was wide open, and I darted

forwards in the split second before it closed. As my boots sped up, I thought I might have accidentally brushed the back of the guard's foot, but he didn't turn around—and I was in.

More werewolf noises followed from outside. *Go on, Alissa. Lead them on a wild weregoose chase.*

The jail was as dark and cramped as ever. I whipped my wand out and cast a silencing spell, the one Alissa often used on our flat when we practised magic. I wanted to seal the door from behind to give myself more time, but that would be a dead giveaway, so I settled for conjuring a small floating light that resembled one of the guards' torches. For some reason, it glittered like a miniature disco ball, but it did the job.

I crept between the row of cells. The front area of the prison was used for petty criminals or people accused of minor crimes, kept overnight as a deterrent. Half the cells were full. Apparently, a lot of people needed deterring from petty crime. I didn't really need the light, because my sixth sense insisted on bombarding me with constant images of each criminal's paranormal type—goblin, witch, wizard, even the odd siren, kept in a tank inside a cell so they didn't die from lack of water. I kept walking between the rows of cells until I reached a sign saying, "HIGH SECURITY THIS WAY."

The door was sealed. This must be the place where they kept murderers and career criminals. I held my hovering light over the door, trying to see if it was sealed with magic or some other mechanism. Looked like it was warded in the same manner as Madame Grey's office. I waved my wand and cast another silencing spell in case any alarms went off. Then I tried an unlocking spell. The door didn't budge. Worth a try.

Problem: I hadn't seen Veronica yet, which must mean she must be behind that door, with the murderers and other serious criminals.

"Who are you?" a voice hissed from behind the bars on my right. "You're not a gargoyle."

No, I'm not. Think, Blair. I hadn't got this far to be defeated by a door. The defences couldn't be *that* sophisticated, otherwise the gargoyles would never be able to get in and out. And they had to frequently enter the jail to feed the prisoners or bring new ones in. The prison did have a back entrance—maybe I should have used that one instead.

A horrible snarling noise came from close by, and one of the doors trembled. Oh, no. I'd woken a werewolf. And it was the full moon outside.

"Shh," I whispered.

The wolf snarled. Inspiration struck, and I backed up until I was out of the werewolf's line of sight.

There came the sound of footsteps. Oh, no. The gargoyle was back, and he was between me and the way out.

Sorry about this.

I waved my wand at the shaking cell door, which burst open. The werewolf exploded out and ran down the corridor with a roar, tasting freedom. Gargoyles exclaimed in alarm, waking the other inmates and sparking a frenzy of noise. Meanwhile, I moved back to the closed security door and hammered on it with all my strength. If I couldn't open it myself, whoever was patrolling in there would doubtless hear the racket inside here.

Sure enough, the door opened, and I shrank against the wall to avoid being hit by the gargoyle's wings. "What's going on in here?" he demanded, surveying the rampaging werewolf and the panicking guards.

I held my breath, waiting out of sight, but the racket was so loud, I could have clumped through wearing doc martens and he wouldn't have heard. As the door hung open for a moment, I darted through it and into the high security area of the prison.

Bare walls and a stale smell greeted me. So this was the realm of the long-term prisoners. I shivered in the chill breeze and ran to the nearest cell door. The barred windows were even smaller than in the other section of the jail, though the cells themselves were larger. And warded, with magic. At least the conditions were a little better than the overnight cells.

"Blair," whispered a familiar voice. "What are you doing in here?"

Veronica. I ran to the door the voice had come from. I couldn't even see her behind the bars. "How did you know it was me?"

"I had an instinct," said Veronica. "Blair, you should leave."

"I can't believe they locked you up with the murderers," I whispered. "Please, I need to know. Were you under a mind-control spell earlier? Have you made eye contact with Simeon—"

"Quiet," she hissed. "It's dangerous for you to be here. There's a door at the back, on the right. Go."

"But..." I backed up from her cell. But I'd come here to

talk to Simeon or Mrs Dailey, not Veronica, and the gargoyle guard would be back at any moment.

I ran to the next cell, my paranormal sixth sense telling me there was a werefox in there. The next was a goblin. I kept moving, certain I'd know when I saw him—then my light shone on his face. Simeon Clarke was barely recognisable, pressed against the bars on the door, but it was undeniably him. I stilled, my heart pounding. He was so close, I was sure he could see my face.

"You," I said. "You used your magic on Veronica, didn't you?"

Simeon didn't move. His face was squashed against the bars in an unnatural, odd pose. And… my ability hadn't reacted to him. *That* was odd.

"Simeon?"

He didn't move. I couldn't touch him through the bars, but cold emanated from his cell. With a wave of my wand, I cast an unlocking spell, but nothing happened.

There came the sound of the security door opening behind me. I swore under my breath and backed up down the row of cells. As the gargoyle's footsteps grew louder, I shrank backwards, spotting the door Veronica had pointed out. It was locked, but seemed to be the only way outside.

The gargoyle's footsteps echoed. I moved toward the door, my heart sinking. I hadn't even found Mrs Dailey, and Simeon…

"He's dead!" roared the gargoyle, and I ran for my life.

This time, my unlocking spell worked on the first try, and I burst out of the back doors, no longer caring if anyone saw. My heart hammered against my ribcage, my steps frantic—and I crashed so hard into a solid form, I saw stars. Reeling back, I tripped into a bush. Ow. That wasn't a gargoyle. He was a man, crouched in the bushes behind the back of the jail.

He jumped away from me. "Who's there?" he said, his voice high and reedy. "Are you a ghost sent to punish me for my sins?"

"What are you doing back here?" I hissed back. "Who are you?"

The light through the closing jail door fell on his face.

Impossible.

It was Dr Appleton.

The moment I gasped, he began to run—unsteadily, like he was drunk or in pain. I scrambled to my feet, brambles snagging my clothes and tangling around my invisible feet. By the time I freed myself, he was gone. I ran forwards a few steps, hardly able to believe what I'd seen. From his face, he'd felt the same. He'd probably thought the ghost of a former prisoner had crashed into him. Unless I was the one who'd run into a ghost. Dr Appleton was supposed to be dead.

And now Simeon was, too.

The door crashed open again, jolting me to attention. The gargoyle had lumbered out of the jail's back door, swearing loudly. Time to go.

Simeon was dead. Had Mrs Dailey killed him? No way. Her wand was gone, and you'd think the police would take basic precautions to ensure nobody could commit murder from inside a cell. It seemed a bare minimum thing to do. Even for Steve. On the other hand, the last dead man I'd encountered had just accused me of being a ghost sent to punish him for his sins.

Hysterical laughter rose in my throat and I pressed a

hand to my mouth, approaching the main road as fast as my boots allowed me to. Picking up speed, I flipped over in surprise when a hand grabbed me from behind.

"Don't fly off!" said Alissa's frantic voice. "I can't see you as it is."

"Ah." I hung awkwardly in the air, unable to figure out how to turn the right way up. Then I found my feet.

"Ow!" said Alissa. "You kicked me in the face."

"Sorry!" I yelped, flipping over and face-planting spectacularly. "Oh. Ow."

"Blair, are you okay?"

"Don't scare me like that," I mumbled, my face throbbing.

"I thought you heard me."

"I can hear you, but I can't see my own face." I touched my nose gingerly. "I think my nose is bleeding."

"Yes, it is." Best hurry up and get home."

"Just what I needed." I tipped my head back, grimacing, and floated along the road. "Er, Alissa?"

"Right here. Keep moving. There's floating blood on your invisible face and it's freaking me out. I think the potion's wearing off."

"Wonderful." I kept floating, trying to keep my head tipped back to stop myself from dripping blood on the ground and only half succeeding.

Alissa unlocked the door to the house and I fell into the hall, landing on top of her in a tangle of invisible limbs.

"Ah!" I scrambled backwards, searching for my keys, but Alissa got there first. The door clicked open, and I waited to be sure Alissa was out of the way of the door before following her in.

Yowling struck up from two corners of the flat. "Oh, hey, Roald," said Alissa. "Blair's going to help you now."

"When I stop bleeding," I mumbled. "Hope nobody saw me from the windows. They'll be having nightmares about ghosts dripping blood."

"Lovely image." The sofa creaked as Alissa flung herself onto it. "Please tell me you at least managed to get something useful in there."

"Nope," I said, pressing a wad of tissue to my nose. "Simeon's dead." *And Dr Appleton's alive.*

I almost heard her jaw drop. "No way."

"Yep. How could someone have killed him from inside the jail?"

"I don't know." Her voice was faint. "You didn't give away that you were there, did you?"

"Only Veronica knew, I think," I said. "But she wouldn't tell me a thing. And I didn't see Mrs Dailey at all. I think they knew someone broke in, though. I wasn't really subtle with my escape."

"If someone's dead in there, I think they have bigger problems."

Unless they found out about my escapade. Then I'd be joining Veronica in a cell. And on top of all that, we had to spend the night being haunted by a pair of invisible cats. Maybe the full moon was bad luck to more than just werewolves.

The following morning dawned cold, grey, and not at all summery. It fit my mood pretty well. After a long, frustrating night, I'd finally managed to turn the cats visible again in the early hours of the morning, but Sky had vanished immediately afterwards and didn't even poke me in the face to wake me up.

Not that I had anywhere to go that morning. I'd failed to achieve anything useful at the jail, and now the person I'd suspected was dead. *And why did Dr Appleton show up outside the jail?* If not for the pile of bloody tissues on the table and Sky's absence, I might have thought I'd imagined the whole night.

My phone rang as I was making coffee. "Bethan," I said, picking it up. "Hi."

"Blair," she said. "Were you at the jail last night?"

"You guessed?"

"It's all over town that that wizard murderer you caught a few months ago committed suicide in there."

"Committed—what?"

"That's the story," said Bethan. "I'm assuming you know what really went on?"

"Nope," I admitted. "I expected to find him alive. He used his ability on Veronica. Why would he kill himself now?" Because he was afraid of getting caught? Or had Mrs Dailey committed murder through the locked door of a cell?

There was a pause, then Bethan said, "Used *what* on Veronica?"

"Mind powers." I drew in a breath. "When she was at the trial yesterday, I noticed Veronica was acting weird. It took me a while to remember, but it's exactly how Blythe looked when Simeon had her under mind control. Since they're at the same jail, and so's Mrs Dailey, I went for a look around last night and found him dead in his cell."

"You're really lucky you weren't caught," said Bethan. "Since nobody was found near the murder scene with a weapon, they're ruling it as a suicide."

But they know there was a break-in. And I wasn't the only intruder there. "Uh, how'd you know I broke in, then?"

"I figured any disturbance at the jail had your name written all over it."

"It was a mistake, and I didn't even find out anything useful. The police didn't suspect I was there, did they?"

"Not that I know of. His murder was all they were talking about when I went there to plead on Veronica's behalf again this morning. I heard Simeon died hours before they found him, so you're probably in the clear, but don't tell that to Steve."

My shoulders slumped in relief. "Good enough. I mean, it's *not* good. Last night was pretty much a disaster, actually." Even if I discounted the invisible cats, the nose-bleed, or nearly giving Alissa a concussion.

"Sounds like it," Bethan said. "A werewolf got out and went ballistic, and several other prisoners escaped in the confusion, too. Anyway, they caught everyone and returned them to their cells. Did… did you see her?"

"Veronica?" I said. "Yes, but she didn't have time to tell me anything. I didn't see how Simeon died either. But—I ran into someone behind the jail when I got outside. Someone who looked like Dr Appleton."

Bethan gave an uncertain laugh. "The dead guy?"

"I literally ran into him in the dark, but he took off like a bat out of hell when I tried to talk to him. Then the gargoyles showed up and I had to run."

"Seriously?" she said. "But… he's dead. I mean, they haven't had the funeral yet, but I think the vampires would have noticed if he'd risen from the grave."

"It looked like him, anyway," I said. "So did you try to speak to Steve again?"

"I tried," she said. "He won't listen, and he's postponed Veronica's appeal because of those hunters visiting. Next time you try to break in, do tell me, won't you?"

"I will, but I don't think I'll get lucky twice," I said.

"Just be careful. If it *is* Mrs Dailey, she must have someone on the outside, too."

Yeah. The assassin. Or Dr Appleton? If it was really him, and he'd killed Simeon… that opened up another lot of questions. Why fake his death? Had *he* wanted to frame Veronica? Whatever the reason, it made no sense for him to wander over to the police station if he wanted people to think he was dead.

My phone buzzed. "Er, I've got another call coming in. Let me know how it goes."

"Sure thing."

Bethan hung up, while I checked who was calling —Nathan.

"Hey, Nathan," I said.

"Blair," he said. "I heard there was a ruckus at the jail last night."

"You might say that." Sighing, I ran through the whole story again. While I did so, Roald entered the kitchen, gave me a reproachful look, and ran off.

"I suppose it might have been worse," Nathan said.

"Considering I turned both cats invisible, the guy I suspected of putting a spell on Veronica is dead and I ran into the person whose murder she was locked up for to begin with, the only way it could have gone worse is if I'd ended up in a cell of my own."

"The good news is you're not a suspect," Nathan told me. "I've just been talking to Steve and he mentioned your name once, but Clare shot him down."

Maybe I was growing on the grumpy receptionist. Though it helped that Simeon had died hours before I'd been there, apparently without anyone noticing. I just wished I could report Dr Appleton's appearance without admitting where I'd been last night. I'd seen *someone* out there, and even if it'd been a disguise, dressing up as a dead man wasn't exactly low-profile.

"I was totally invisible," I said to Nathan. "Nobody but Veronica heard me speak. And Simeon, but you know, he's dead."

"Good," he said. "Simeon's death, though—they ruled it a suicide purely because nobody else could have got into the cell. It looks like he fell and hit his head, and it would normally be blamed on a spell, but his cell was sealed and so were the doors."

"I think I know who did it," I said.

"Blair, are you absolutely certain it was Dr Appleton you saw?"

"No, I'm not. The person I ran into was definitely alive, but it was dark and he might have used an illusion spell. Has he been buried yet?"

"I believe the funeral's this week," he said. "But I wouldn't tell Steve what you saw. There's no excuse you have for being anywhere near the jail last night."

"Figures," I said. "It's Mr Falconer all over again. I thought they'd put measures into place to stop anyone from trying the same thing." I hadn't exactly been on top of things lately, but you'd think making sure the victim was actually dead would be the police's priority.

"I thought they had, too," he said. "I saw Dr Appleton's body myself, actually, and they had Madame Grey look at it in person. She'd have seen through any deception."

Huh. "Then maybe it was someone using an illusion spell. Like Simeon's killer. He said something weird about me being a ghost sent to punish him for his sins, but that's because I crashed into him while invisible."

"Really, Blair." I could almost see him shaking his head at me on the other end of the phone. "I'd normally advise you to find a way to alert the authorities without giving away your own presence, but considering the state of things, it's best to wait until the hunters are gone."

"Wait, they're here now?"

"I thought you knew," he said. "They're speaking to Madame Grey right now."

My heart dropped unpleasantly. "Seriously? I didn't know they'd be coming this soon."

"I would have preferred it if they'd warned me, too." He sounded frustrated, and I didn't blame him. "They're interviewing the council, I believe, but I don't know how many other inspections they plan to carry out."

There was a rapping on the flat door. "Someone's here to see me."

"Okay. I'll talk to you later, Blair. Take care of yourself."

He ended the call, while I went to the window to see who was there.

A huge gargoyle stood on the doorstep. Steve. Oh, no.

Alissa walked out of the bathroom, casting a drying spell on her hair with a swift flick of her wand. "Who is it?"

"Steve." I cast a wild look around the flat. "What if he wants to look in here for proof of anything dodgy?"

"There's no traces of the invisibility potion left," she said. "He can't prove a thing."

The door rattled at another knock. "Better let him in before he knocks the door down."

I hurried to the door, hoping he wasn't here to arrest me after all. *Please tell me I'm not being accused of Simeon's murder.* That was all I needed.

I opened the door, feigning astonishment. "Steve. To what do I owe the pleasure?"

"Don't use that tone with me," he growled. "I'm here to question you about a murder."

I blinked innocently. "I thought you already ruled that Veronica killed Dr Appleton."

"Not that murder," he snapped. "Someone broke into the jail and killed Simeon Clarke."

I schooled my face into a contrite expression. "Nathan just called me to tell me."

His scowl didn't waver. "He told you of the break-in last night too, then?"

"Yeah, but he said Simeon died hours before it happened." Now would be the perfect time to tell him of my suspicions that Veronica hadn't been entirely in control of her actions during the trial… if the perpetrator wasn't dead. Was Mrs Dailey covering her tracks, or was there more than one killer out there?

"You're up to something, Blair Wilkes. Give me one good reason why I shouldn't lock you up."

"Because I haven't committed a crime, and you can't throw everyone in jail if they annoy you. Even the hunters know that. Aren't you supposed to be meeting with them?"

"At their discretion," he growled. "Your interfering partner in crime insisted on informing me of that this morning."

He and Nathan must have had an argument as well. "Look, I'm sorry the hunters are here, but it's hardly my fault. It's technically Mrs Dailey's. I'm sure she has someone running around on her behalf—"

"Enough," he snapped. "I won't listen to any more of your excuses, Blair Wilkes, and I will not lose my position to these *normals*."

So it was the hunters who'd ticked him off, then.

Steve gave me a last ugly look and left while I closed the door, my hands shaking. "Guess I should be glad he doesn't *support* the hunters."

"You're popular today," Alissa commented.

"Not with Steve." I returned to the living room. "He's just throwing around accusations left and right because he's scared of the hunters kicking him off his pedestal."

"I don't blame him, considering the reputation this Inquisitor Hare has. I didn't know he was already here, but it explains why Madame Grey isn't answering my messages." Alissa scratched Roald between the ears, reminding me of the conspicuous absence of my own cat. Sky would forgive me eventually, and the one thing that'd gone right last night was that I'd figured out how to glamour someone invisible. Even if I hadn't used it on myself yet.

Maybe I should go and ask Dr Summers if she was aware that her ex-husband might be alive after all. Or at least that someone was running around pretending to be him. But with no proof, she'd think I was bonkers. Assuming the two of them hadn't been working together...

My phone went off again. "Maybe you're right," I told Alissa. "Everyone wants a piece of me today. Hello... Madame Grey?"

"Blair," she said. "I'd like you to come and talk to the hunters. Inquisitor Hare has requested to speak to you."

"He did?" The leader of the paranormal hunters wanted to talk to *me?*

"He knows about your power, Blair, and wants to see a demonstration."

Oh, boy. That couldn't mean anything good.

10

I walked to the witches' headquarters, trying unsuccessfully to put on my best professional face. The hunters needed to get the best impression of the town possible, so they'd see that we were doing just fine without their help. But my thoughts swirled out of control. Why would the Inquisitor want a demonstration of my lie-sensing powers? He didn't know me. I was pretty sure I'd recall if I'd ever met the person who owned the hunters' jail.

The person who'd jailed my father.

Silence filled the lobby when I entered, but the door to the main meeting room was partly open and the murmur of voices came from within. Drawing in a breath, I entered.

Madame Grey stood at one end of the table that dominated the room, while the other coven members filled one side. The table's other side was occupied by the hunters, including Sleepy, Dopey and Grumpy. I'd picked their nicknames well. Sleepy was tall and thin and had a perpetually tired expression. Grumpy wore an angry scowl and his shaved head reflected the ceiling lights. Dopey, meanwhile, was shorter and stockier with thick dark hair, and constantly looked confused at the world in general.

My gaze fell on the man sitting at the opposite end of the table, and I forgot all about the hunters. He wore a pressed suit, not dirty rugged hiking gear like the other hunters. His frame was tall and strong, his movements smooth and confident, and there was something animalistic in his gaze when his charcoal-black eyes turned in my direction. My paranormal sensing power kicked into gear, showing me images of… blank walls?

What's it reacting to? Was Inquisitor Hare not human? If he wasn't, then what was he? Something my ability didn't recognise? Nobody had told me he was paranormal. I'd thought the hunters were all human. Aggressively so. Whatever he was, though, every one of my instincts told me he was dangerous. Very dangerous.

"Blair, take a seat," said Madame Grey. "We were just getting started."

"Yes, we were," said the Inquisitor, finally turning to me. My blood iced over. His stare was cunning and penetrating, and my paranormal sensing powers bounced off a brick wall. *Ow.* I hadn't had a reaction that strong even when I'd looked at a vampire or gargoyle shifter. I broke away from his gaze and took the only available seat. Luckily, it was between two witches, as far as possible from Inquisitor Hare.

"Hello," I said to him. "I'm Blair. You're Inquisitor

Hare, right?" The best thing to do was to act harmless. And like he didn't scare me.

"I am," he said. "I heard you had an unusual talent."

"I—which talent?" I suspected I knew which, but his immunity to my paranormal-sensing power threw me. It'd only got confused before when I ran into ghosts, humans transformed into mice, or someone who was two types of paranormal at once. Like a wizard turned into a vampire. But even then, I'd had a result. For him, I might as well have tried to use my power on a painting or photograph. A painting that stared back like a caged beast. *This is a bad idea. A really bad idea.*

"Which one?" He arched a brow. "Interesting. I refer to your remarkable ability to sense lies. Since I'm conducting an inspection, I need someone impartial to tell me if your fellow townspeople are attempting to mask the truth."

True... lie.

Huh? Was he immune to my truth-sensing power, too? That couldn't be right.

He gave me a look to indicate I was supposed to speak. "Yes," I said. "I can sense whether or not someone is lying."

"Good," he said, like he was a schoolteacher giving me a lecture. Unlike Rita or Madame Grey, his tone came across as distinctly patronising, and hidden with meaning, like he was in on a secret that I wasn't. I wouldn't have liked him even if he was human.

"You want me to test if *you're* lying?" I asked, then regretted it.

"That's not necessary." Again, his words came laced with meaning. He *knew* I couldn't tell if he was lying or not. "We'll resume the meeting."

"Yes, we shall," said Madame Grey, projecting all the authority she had in her. "Let's get this over with, Inquisitor. I'm sure you have other important business to handle."

"Your town intrigues me," he said. "I have to admit, Fairy Falls slipped off my radar until I heard rumour of a rabid wolf who contacted the office."

"No such thing occurred," Madame Grey said. "The town was affected last week by an unexpected spell when a witch who'd formerly demonstrated no talent was found to have a very rare form of magic, the ability to affect the personalities of other townspeople. That included the werewolf in question, who has now returned to normal."

"You were affected yourself, correct?" he said, before I could verify she spoke true. It was like he'd forgotten about me.

"Yes," she said, matter-of-factly. "The witch in question managed to reverse the spell and her mother, who was manipulating her talent, is now in custody. She was found to have allowed three of your people to enter the town without permission." She indicated Sleepy, Dopey and Grumpy.

"As I'm to understand it, they found nobody guarding the border," Inquisitor Hare said.

"That's not true," I said. "Mrs Dailey knocked the guards out herself."

"That sounds like an error on your part rather than ours, Miss Wilkes," he said, without blinking, apparently unsurprised by the interruption. "I believe you worked for the office which called the paranormal hunters' headquarters? Your voice is on the recorded message."

"Yes, I did," I said, certain he was trying to intimidate

me. I'd had enough of that from Steve this week already. "Unfortunately, their call to the office happened to coincide with my co-worker falling under the spell."

His sharp black eyes made me want to shrivel up in my seat. I risked a glance at Madame Grey, and only her encouraging nod made me stay put.

"Your co-worker," he repeated. "This Eldritch & Co does seem to be connected to your considerable security problems, doesn't it? You hired the current security team?"

Why was he so interested? He could have asked anyone in town, but for some reason, he'd chosen me. And not for my lie-sensing skills, I was almost certain of it.

"Yes, I did. They'll stop any trespassers." I pointedly looked at Grumpy, Sleepy and Dopey, but none of them appeared particularly concerned.

"Assuming your town isn't bewitched by a single person again," he said. "A child at that."

"As I said, she's a child who didn't know her limits and was manipulated," Madame Grey said. "Her mother, naturally, is in jail."

"So, I hear, is Ms Eldritch."

Ah.

"Yes," said Madame Grey. "She found the body of a murdered trespasser in her office and was arrested as a consequence. She did, however, plead innocent, and the case is ongoing."

"Interesting," he said. "I would question the value of anyone hired by a murderer."

I bit my tongue, fighting the impulse to point out that

it was hardly better than inviting hunters into town who'd been hired by someone who might be a murderer for all we knew. Who knew how many other crimes Mrs Dailey had committed before she'd been caught? She'd evaded attention for that long, after all. And she'd been in contact with the hunters for a while.

"I was the one who hired them," I said, struggling to keep my tone calm. "And as Madame Grey said, the case is ongoing. I happen to think my employer is innocent, but that's neither here nor there."

"Did I hear someone died at the jail last night?" he said.

"A suicide," said one of the other hunters. "Or so they claim, anyway."

"Nothing like that has ever happened at any of our institutes," he said. "I do question the efficiency of small towns' resources like this one, particularly ones who insist on remaining independent."

"What are you implying?" Madame Grey said. "We have a very low crime rate and are working on expanding our security forces to include those with an array of talents. I rather think the last thing we need is more change."

"I suppose you know best," said Inquisitor Hare, and I bristled. Was he playing to the part of the council who wanted to unseat Madame Grey? Or was he just trying to make himself and the hunters look better than she was? "If you change your mind, there's always room at the Lancashire Prison for Paranormals."

His head tilted in my direction, just a little.

I stiffened. I was sure he'd directed that comment at me. He *did* know my dad was there.

"Naturally," said Madame Grey, not cowed in the slightest. "That said, I'm surprised that the leader of the highest office of the paranormal hunters would need to involve himself in the affairs of a small town like ours."

"For a small town, you certainly seem shrouded in rumours," he said. "Beasts living in the woods, border transgressions, a werewolf in an office, the town's leader falling under a child's spell…"

Madame Grey looked like she wanted to strangle him. She was also the only person on the witches' side of the room who didn't look intimidated by Inquisitor Hare's presence. He was one scary man.

"I think you've made your views clear," Madame Grey said. "And I see no need to make changes to how we run things."

"You seem certain," he commented. "Very well, we'll end things here."

He was acting like he'd dismissed the meeting, not her. Annoyance seized me, but everyone else got to their feet and began to file out. Probably, they wanted to get away from the guy. So did I—but suddenly he was at my side, beckoning to me.

Every inch of me froze up. I did *not* want to be alone in the room with him. Possibly even less than Blythe's mother, and that was saying a lot. Faced with him this close, though—I didn't dare make a run for it. Madame Grey was just outside the room, after all.

"Blair, I'll let you in on a secret," he said, dropping his voice. "We do in fact employ many witches and wizards at our facility. Non-paranormals only make up a fraction of our forces. I heard you haven't been part of the para-normal world for long, and this town is the extent of your experience. If you want to try out a new way of life, the hunters are always open for new recruits. Your unique skillset would make you an asset. I'd invite you to consider it."

He wants to hire me?

Somehow, I managed to unstick my tongue from the roof of my mouth. "No, thank you," I said. "I don't think it's for me. Besides, I have a job."

"Yes, for now," he said. "I do hope the council makes the right decision."

"I think they're making the right decision in telling you to leave," I said, my hand on the door. "Thank you for your time."

This time I fled before he could waylay me again, my heart hammering in my chest. The witches had dispersed through the entrance hall. Dr Summers included. I'd been too fixated on Inquisitor Hare to notice her presence in the meeting. Should I tell her I thought I'd seen her dead husband? Since he'd run off, there was a fair chance that she'd think I was nuts. Besides, if I admitted I'd been near the jail, then she'd draw her own conclusions. I hadn't ruled out her being on Mrs Dailey's side yet. With the hunters still here, the last thing I needed was more conflict.

I crossed the lobby to the doors and found Nathan waiting outside.

"I heard," he said, his expression concerned. "I didn't know he'd want to see you in person."

"Nor me." I released a breath. "Do you know him? Inquisitor Hare?"

"He's in charge of every prison in the region," he said. "That technically makes him my family's boss. I didn't think he involved himself in this type of thing—not a small town like this."

"That's what Madame Grey said, too." I moved away from the doors. "He's here, though—and so are Sleepy, Dopey and Grumpy. You know, the three morons we ran into in the woods."

"Oh, them," he said. "No, they're who I'd expected to show up, since they work for the same branch of the hunters that I did. They *don't* work for the LFPF. I don't know why Inquisitor Hare showed up instead of the leader of the local hunters' branch. It's not typical."

"He knows me," I said. "He knew about my powers."

"Madame Grey told him. She had to."

"But did he ask?" My hands clenched at my sides. "He *knew* me."

"Blair, this isn't the place to talk. Maybe we should go somewhere quieter."

"Sure." I gave the doors a last uneasy look. "He seriously creeped me out."

My heart rate steadied as we left the witches' headquarters behind. Charms & Caffeine was too close for my liking, so I picked out the café in the back of the bookshop where we'd first been on a 'date'. It was also where I'd found Sky. I couldn't help scanning the shelves for a glimpse of his white paw and loud 'miaow'.

"What is it, Blair?" asked Nathan, spotting me staring at the shelves. "Did you want to get something from the shop?"

"No." I shook my head. "My cat's angry with me. I thought he might have come here, but he's probably with Vincent."

Did the vampire know the hunters were in town?

Wait… I should have noticed, but the only people who'd been in the meeting had been the witches and wizards who ran the covens. No non-human paranormals aside from a couple of gargoyles. Weird.

"Why's Sky angry with you?" asked Nathan.

"Because I turned him invisible last night when I was trying to figure out how to use my glamour," I said. "I ended up using my glamour on the cats instead. That's partly why last night was such a disaster—I didn't have Sky with me." I kept my voice low, wishing we'd gone to a more private place, but there didn't seem to be anyone around among the dusty shelves. Maybe everyone had run from the hunters' presence. The only other people in the cafe were a group of serious-looking wizardly businessmen who looked like the type who might have once hired Dritch & Co.

How had things gone downhill so quickly?

I ordered a calming smoothie rather than my usual mood-bolstering coffee, figuring I needed calmness more than caffeine. Nathan ordered coffee, the extra strong kind.

"I'll likely be on the night shift again," he said in explanation. "The gargoyles are assisting me with training the new security guards, but they can't become experts overnight, and if we're to pass the hunters' inspection, they'll have to at least pretend to be."

"Argh," I said, sipping my smoothie. Maybe I should have taken a double dose, even if it knocked me out cold. My whole body was wound tight with stress. "It's a pain. I don't know Inquisitor Hare at all, but he acted like he knew me, and it creeped me out. And he's—I'm certain he's paranormal."

He looked at me sharply. "Are you sure?"

"He set off my powers, but they went blank. Like he's something they don't recognise, or he's blocking them in some way. He wanted to *recruit* me."

His eyes widened. "You didn't say yes?"

"Of course not. I don't know why he'd want me to join the hunters. He sort of implied it was to do with my lie-sensing power, but he didn't ask for a proper demonstration. It's like he wanted an excuse for me to see him give the council a talking-down. Which makes no sense. I mean, he doesn't know me."

He gave me a serious look. "No, he shouldn't. Nor should he be here. I've only met him a handful of times while I was a hunter. He didn't often visit our branch. But…"

"But what?"

"He was there the day they brought your father in. Needless to say, I didn't actually speak to him…"

"But he knew. I guess that's why. The Inquisitor locked my dad up and now he wants me. Why?"

"I don't know," he said. "Maybe he was testing your reaction. What did he say?"

"That this town gave me a lopsided view of the paranormal world and I was welcome to join the hunters, or something. A recruitment speech. Is that how they sell it to recruits?"

"I was born into it," he reminded me. "And I certainly didn't know he was in the habit of singling people out from towns like this one. It's not common for people to leave Fairy Falls at all, let alone to work for the hunters. And as far as I know, he's generally much too busy to recruit people in person."

Then why me? Considering my dad was in jail, it made no sense for him to want the daughter of a pair of alleged criminals on his side. Unless the hunters were desperate for people with lie-sensing powers to work for them. *Not happening.*

I looked down at my smoothie. "I said no to him. Will that get me into trouble? Or you?"

"It shouldn't," he said. "No, I can't say I know why he asked you, but he must have expected you'd be wary of the hunters."

"I can't help feeling like it's my fault for calling the hunters in the first place," I admitted, slumping in my seat.

"It wasn't you, Blair," he said.

"It was Mrs Dailey." I absently stirred my drink. "It was all her. I know I sound paranoid—heaven knows Steve won't believe me, and I can't tell the hunters *that*—but I feel like she's engineering this. She has people working for her outside the jail and there's no way to *prove* it."

"Maybe there is," he said. "But I won't be allowed to help you with anything illegal. It's too risky. If I were to lose my own job or credibility, the hunters would be able to entirely take over the town's security."

I grimaced. "I'm not asking you to involve yourself, but I don't know where to go from here. I can't break into the jail again, and who's going to believe I saw the man who's supposed to be dead? Even being able to sense lies isn't enough for the police, and..."

"And what?"

I drew in a breath. "I can block people from my mind. Most people with mind powers, except Vincent, I think. So I can't even get someone else to verify whether or not *I'm* telling the truth."

He was quiet for a moment. "Would Vincent back you up?"

"No chance," I said. "Okay, maybe one percent of a chance. Is it worth talking to him?"

"I'd say it is," he said. "We'll go to see Vincent."

11

Nathan wanted to go with me to see the head of the vampires? The world really had flipped upside-down. Nathan had made no secret of the fact that he disliked the elder vampire—possibly in part because of the mind-reading thing. He wasn't the jealous type, but vampires had a well-known reputation for seducing people, if just to drink their blood. Not to mention their uncanny ability to appear from nowhere must be irritating for a security guard to deal with.

I had to admit the weirdest thing about Vincent was his friendship with my cat. Maybe I'd get lucky and find him there. Poor Sky. He knew my magical skill was questionable and that I hadn't meant to put the glamour on him, so he must be sulking somewhere. He'd forgive me eventually.

Vincent answered when I rapped on the door, appearing on the doorstep as though my knock had summoned him from thin air.

"Blair Wilkes," he said. "What brings you here?"

"Hey, Vincent. Have you seen my cat?" I asked. "We had a… a misunderstanding last night."

"Is that so?" he said. "And am I to assume that's the only reason you came here, and not to ask for a favour?"

I blinked at his irritable tone. "Not a favour. I kind of wanted advice, actually. What should I do when I know something is true and nobody else will believe me, even if it could get an innocent woman out of jail? You can verify I'm telling the truth, right?"

"Not necessarily," he said. "Mind-reading has its limits, and besides, I might lie as easily as you."

Nathan stepped in. "If I may add to Blair's request, the town is currently under inspection by the paranormal hunters. Both of us believe they were brought here by the word of someone who's currently incarcerated. Needless to say, the police refuse to take our word for it."

I gave him a sideways glance. He'd suggested to Steve that Blythe's mother might be behind the hunters' presence here? No wonder Steve was hopping mad at him.

"That's unfortunate," said Vincent. "I confess I'm lost on what you expect *me* to do about it."

"Back us up," I said. "If the hunters take over the town, things won't go well for any of us, so it's in your best interests to help us."

"Exactly," Nathan said. "The hunters would certainly displace the coven's laws where appropriate. Including, perhaps, the rule dictating that vampires who break the rules are allowed to punish their own first, unless the crime is of a severe nature."

There was a flash of fangs. "If that's the case, my people and I will go elsewhere."

"What?" I stepped back. "You'll leave town altogether?

Come on, you must know it's Blythe's mother stirring up trouble again. If I can prove Veronica's innocence—"

"Maybe you can, maybe not," he said. "But there's no reason for the police or the hunters to take my word over their own judgement. I pick my battles, and so do my people."

"You could prove Veronica's innocence in a second."

"Would they believe me?" His teeth became more prominent. He was mad. "And do you think it would endear the gargoyles any more to the hunters if it turns out they locked up the wrong person?"

I threw up my hands in frustration. "No, but an innocent woman is in jail, and I *saw* the person she's accused of murdering. Or someone who looked exactly like him. If I tell the police *that,* they'll think I've lost my mind."

"What a pity," he said blandly, with a glance over his shoulder at the fog-shrouded cemetery on the other side of the vampires' headquarters. "Shame there's no way to prove the truth, is there?"

Was he making fun of me? I opened my mouth to reply, and he said, "I have a summit in ten minutes. Please refrain from bothering me in future unless it's an emergency."

And he closed the door.

"It *is* an emergency," I said to the blank stretch of oak wood. "Great."

"We should leave," said Nathan.

Fuming, I marched alongside Nathan. "Talking to him is like repeatedly hitting myself over the head with a broomstick. I can't believe he's going to run off if the hunters take over."

"He might not be entirely truthful," said Nathan. "Didn't he pull a similar stunt in the council meeting?"

"He didn't set off my lie detector," I said. "Which means yes, he does plan to do a runner and leave the rest of us to sort the mess out on our own. He didn't even tell me where my cat went."

"No," he said. "But I got the impression he was trying to give you a clue on how to prove the truth. Are you sure it was Dr Appleton you saw?"

"No. If it was an illusion, though, it was a good one," I said. "I mean, I knew he was a wizard when I looked at him, but I wasn't really focusing at the time. Doesn't change anything."

Or did it? I hadn't stopped for long enough to really look at the guy behind the jail, but if he was pretending to be Dr Appleton, he must have had a good reason to. He hadn't been expecting to run into me there in the dark. He'd already been in the jail.

Had *he* killed Simeon? He'd certainly acted guilty. And scared.

"I… I think I should talk to the people Dr Appleton knew again," I said. "It's possible the killer disguised himself as him as a cover, but it's not really the logical thing to do. I'm not convinced he was picked as a victim by accident. He knew Veronica, and his wife's a council member who supports the hunters. She *said* she didn't do it and my lie detector didn't go off, though."

"No, there's certainly something else at work." Nathan frowned. "If there'd been other witnesses… I take it Dr Appleton, or whoever he was, took off as soon as the police showed up?"

"You've got it. Also, he didn't know it was me. I was

still invisible at the time, but I ran smack into him so he knew there was someone around who shouldn't be."

There were ways to tell if someone was invisible… might the same be true of illusions?

"Nathan," I said, as we walked downhill away from the vampires' place. "Can you tell me the hunters' trick for seeing through illusions? I mean, I guess it doesn't work on fairy glamour, but I doubt that's what the killer's using."

His mouth pressed together. "I can't teach you years of training in a day. It's to do with looking for signs. If it *was* an illusion, there'd be a sort of… flicker, out of the corner of your eye. It's a tell that accompanies most spells, but it's more difficult to see in the dark. I think if you have a good eye for it, and most hunters do, it's easier to see."

"I knew I should have grabbed the guy," I muttered. "I think he was Mrs Dailey's personal assassin and he came out of the jail just before I did." After murdering Simeon.

"I don't doubt she has someone on the outside," he said. "But I'm not sure you'll be able to prove they communicated with one another, let alone with the hunters. There's no phone signal in the jail, for a start."

"Then she's using an intermediary. You do believe she's behind this, don't you?"

Nathan took my hand. "Yes, Blair. I believe you. I just think you need to tread carefully around the hunters."

"I'm trying to," I said, squeezing his hand back. "I didn't expect their leader to single me out. He's not the one Mrs Dailey got in touch with, is he? Do they know one another?"

He frowned. "Not that I know of, but I can't say we've spoken much. With her being a known criminal, though, it's extremely unlikely. The three hunters she worked with were pardoned with a caution and shouldn't have been here at all. I'd say it's more likely that he heard about the recent events and chose to come here of his own accord."

To see me. "Mrs Dailey, though… what did you tell Steve about her?"

"I advised him to keep an eye on her. He didn't react well," he said. "I'll try again, but he blames me for the hunters' presence to begin with. But he might listen if I tell him his own job and position might depend on Veronica's innocence."

"And Blythe's mother's scheming," I added. "All right. I won't tick off Steve, but I think I should have a word with Dr Summers again. Even if she isn't involved, someone should probably tell her that a potential assassin is running around disguised as her dead husband."

"If you're sure," he said. "That's probably safer than going back to the witches' headquarters, considering Inquisitor Hare might not have left town yet."

"Mm." I stopped walking, turning back towards the hill. "What about you?"

"I have to go back to my team," he said. "I swear, it won't always be this chaotic. The point of me training so many people at once is that they'll be able to pick up some of the workload. Then we'll get to spend more time together later down the line."

"Can't complain about that, can I?"

He kissed me goodbye. That was enough to improve my mood, and I all but skipped uphill again. I sobered when I passed the vampires' place, wishing I could have convinced Vincent to help. The Inquisitor apparently hadn't wanted to recruit *him*. Or the werewolves, though Chief Donovan would flip a lid when he found out he'd been in town. Assuming he didn't already know.

So the Inquisitor had walked in, ignored every paranormal except for a select group of witches and tried to recruit me. For what purpose? Maybe being able to read minds would come in handy after all. My paranormal-sensing power had its limitations.

It hadn't known what Inquisitor Hare was, after all.

———

When I entered the university campus, my determination began to fade. Maybe I should poke around Dr Appleton's office for signs that he might not be dead before pestering his wife again. Even if it hadn't been him, sooner or later someone else would run into him. Right?

Samuel the vampire greeted me at the library entrance. "Back for more books already?" he asked.

"Uh. Not exactly," I said. "Unless you have a proper guide which can teach me how to use fairy magic?"

Where had that come from? Maybe I *had* lost my wits.

"I can check," he said. "I'm afraid it's not taught at the university, for obvious reasons."

I shook my head. "Never mind. I'm not thinking clearly. Uh, I was looking for—"

"Blair?" Vera, the overenthusiastic assistant from last time, appeared from a row of shelves. "You're back. Did you want to take part in one of the experiments after all? I found some of Dr Appleton's research and I really think it has the potential to go far… pity I couldn't find all of it."

"Dr Appleton's research?" I asked. "Uh, what type of study?"

As she started talking at a mile a minute, I spotted Samuel slinking away behind a shelf. I didn't blame him a bit. It took three false starts before I managed to say, "Uh, Vera, could you explain the study in smaller words? I'm afraid it's been a while since I've been in an academic setting and I'm still at a level two in witch theory."

She slowed to breathe. "Of course I can! The subject of the study was lycanthropy, which is—"

"Werewolves?" I said. "Uh, was he bitten by one of them?"

"I don't *think* so, but he's the type of person who'd get bitten deliberately in the name of research. Not just lycanthropy, though—metamorphosis or transfiguration. Changing something into something else."

"Huh," I said. "That's, er, interesting. Do you think it might be linked to what happened to him?"

"Oh, I doubt it," she said, and resumed her explanation of his study.

My head started to hurt, and finally I cut through her endless stream of one-sided conversation and said, "Was Veronica interested in his study, too?"

"Veronica who?" She blinked as though only just aware that she was talking to a person and not a piece of furniture.

"Eldritch."

"Is she new here?"

"Never mind," I said, deflated. "If I said I saw Dr Appleton the other day, would you believe me?"

"Oh, where?" she asked. "I knew he'd be the type who stuck around after death... too many unfinished experiments. I've been waiting for him to show up and tell me where he hid his notes."

"Not a ghost. I mean, really him." The paranormal world still sometimes took me by surprise sometimes, in that things like ghosts were a matter of course. Now *that* would be an easy way to tell if he was really dead. Pity summoning ghosts on command was either impossible or illegal depending on who you asked. "I saw him walking around the other night. It looked exactly like him."

She blinked. "Maybe you imagined it. You did see his dead body, after all."

At least she'd stopped blathering at me. "Is Dr Summers in?"

"Oh, she's at the council meeting."

I pressed a hand to my forehead. "Right... of course." Madame Grey must have asked the other coven leaders to stay behind after the hunters had left, probably to discuss how to convince them not to come back. "Never mind. I'll see you later."

That's what I got for not thinking my plans through. Let's face it, nobody would believe I'd seen a dead man walking, even in a town of paranormals.

———

"That's it," said Alissa, after I'd told her about the day I'd had. "We're going out tonight. I mean, really out. I'm not working tomorrow and neither are you, so we might as well have some fun with it."

"I could use sanity, not fun." I yawned and lay back on the sofa. Sky still hadn't come back, and despite all the times he'd mocked me or deliberately tried to annoy me, I missed him horribly. "All right, you win."

I'd yet to revive my social life after the incident when I'd first exposed my fairy powers for the world to see, and while my guilt over Veronica's imprisonment remained, I'd achieve nothing by staying at home feeling sorry for myself.

The way things were going, I was as likely to run into Dr Appleton's ghost at the Troll's Tavern than anywhere else.

In the end, I could have run into Dr Appleton riding a dragon wearing a tutu and I wouldn't have the slightest recollection of it in the morning. When Alissa went out, she went all-out. I woke up the following day in a pile of discarded clothes, my head a fuzzy mess, when a cat's claw stabbed me in the cheekbone.

"Ow." I groaned. I was dead. Nope, if I was dead, I wouldn't be in this much pain.

"MIAOW."

I yelped and jumped upright. "Sky! You're back!"

He let out an indignant yowl as I hugged him, managing to get in a good helping of claws. I didn't care, despite my raging headache. Sky hadn't abandoned me after all.

"Miaow," he grumbled.

"Love you too." I heard an incoherent groan from behind Alissa's half-open door. "Sounds like the anti-hangover stuff in the cocktails wore off." Alissa and the other witches had talked me into trying every fairy-themed speciality in the Troll's Tavern. My memory was distorted, but I vaguely recalled several lopsided games of floating air hockey afterwards, and tripping over Leopold passed out in the doorway on the way home.

"Miaow," said Sky.

"Yes, I know I shouldn't try the invisibility thing again," I said, burying my head in his fur. He wriggled free and jumped onto the floor. "At least I know it works."

"Miaow." He gave me another reproachful look.

"What?" I said. "I said I'm sorry for turning you invisible."

"Miaow."

I rolled over and grabbed some witchy painkillers I'd left for myself on the bedside table, swallowing them dry. Then I checked the time. Six in the morning. I wasn't even remotely annoyed, even with the pounding in my head reminding me of the shots I definitely shouldn't have done last night. I hoped the painkillers would kick in soon.

Sky flopped into my space on the bed when I tried to lie back down. I shook my head at him. "You missed all the action again. Did you know the hunters were in town yesterday?"

"Miaow," he said, which might have meant, 'tell me all about your troubles' or alternatively, 'I'm not interested, I'm a cat'. Who knew.

I sat on the edge of the bed. "The leading hunter wants to recruit me and thinks the town's going to the dogs. Veronica is still stuck in jail. Someone killed Simeon Clarke right after I was sure he used mind control on Veronica. And on top of that, Dr Appleton might be alive and I can't *prove* it."

"Miaow." Sky jumped off the bed, padded to the windowsill, and rapped on the glass. There came another groan from Alissa's room.

"Someone outside?" Was the elf back?

Sky tapped on the glass again, and a familiar flash of glitter caught my eye. I grabbed my slippers and keys, leaving my bedroom. With Sky on my heels, I made my way outside into the back garden.

The pixie waited, flitting about. "You could have come in," I said. Probably, he hadn't wanted to disturb me in my fragile state. My headache was fading, though. "Oh—did my dad write back?"

The pixie dropped a note into my hands in response. I read it, my heart racing.

Blair,

You wanted to know about fairy magic. It's a little similar to the witches', but not in every way. Your gift might have come from your mother's side, but I can't say for sure.

However, if you want to change your glamour, you'll need to have your human glamour off and focus strongly on what you want to become.

"Oh," I said. "I have to be in fairy mode to use glamour." You couldn't use two glamours at once, and my human form *was* a glamour. That explained it.

"Miaow."

I looked down at Sky. "I turned you invisible, though. You're glamoured already, right?"

"Miaow," he said.

"Wait, you aren't?" I frowned. "Hang on. Is that your real form? That huge monster is just a glamour?"

Sky licked a paw. Not going to admit it, huh. But I was pretty sure I was right. Well, then.

I turned the note over, but nothing else was written on the other side. Not a word about whether anyone else in my family was still alive. I guess that sort of thing was too risky to put in a letter.

Sky dug his paws into the flowerbed, sending soil flying everywhere.

"What's that for?" I asked him. "Don't ruin the flowerbeds. They're Alissa's."

He kept digging, giving me a look that I'd label as exasperated on a human. Wait, was he trying to communicate with me?

"You want me to dig up… what?"

He flopped onto his back. Playing dead now?

"Very convincing," I told him. "Digging… dead…" The image of the vampires' headquarters came to mind, and Vincent's pointed look over the fence. "I am *not* digging up Dr Appleton's grave to prove he's not dead."

"Miaow." Sky flipped upright and shook soil off his claws.

"Tell me that's not what you meant."

"Miaow."

Oh, no. Yes, my cat *was* telling me to go and dig up a dead body. Wait, had they even had the funeral yet? I'd need to check, but I was sure it was meant to be this week…

Wait. Vincent had been trying to tell me something, too. Had he meant the same? Surely not. As a vampire, he was used to dealing with dead bodies… and he'd definitely know if someone wasn't really dead.

More to the point, I was fairly sure the vampires owned the local mortuary, and some of them were in charge of preparing the dead for burial. And the ban on using magic on the dead was so stringent, I'd heard it said that they kept the bodies of the recent dead in the basement of the…

"That crafty snake," I said. "Was he seriously inviting me to break into the vampires' headquarters?" If the funeral hadn't taken place yet, Dr Appleton would be in a coffin right there. Checking he was really dead would be easy.

On the other hand, if I got it wrong, I might end up with a bunch of angry vamps on my tail if I broke into their headquarters. I didn't want to get arrested for grave-robbing on top of everything else.

I looked up at the sun. While daylight didn't cause vampires to burst into flame like the legends said, they were known to be creatures of the night who slept at dawn.

"I'll only do this if you back me up," I said to Sky.

"Miaow."

12

I can't believe I'm doing this.

Grave-robbing, and breaking into the vampires' headquarters, with my cat. I was far from a stellar example of good behaviour at the best of times, but this week was really testing my resolve not to break more laws than the actual criminals.

I snapped my fingers to turn off my glamour and spread my wings wide to fly up close to the clouds. I hadn't had nearly as much time to enjoy my newfound talents as I would have liked, and I couldn't resist swooping around a bit. If I ran into anyone, I could just say I'd gone for an early morning flight. Say 'it's a fairy thing', and it could be an excuse for anything. If I got caught breaking into the vampires' place and opening coffins, though, it was pretty safe to say I'd be back to square one. Assuming they didn't just lock me in a coffin of my own and throw away the key.

I flew lower as I reached the top of the hill near the

vampires' place. Sky sat waiting below one of the windows. Unsurprisingly, the blinds were down.

I pulled out my wand. "Is anyone awake in there?" I whispered to Sky.

"Miaow." He jerked his head, which meant no. I took in a deep breath and cast an unlocking spell on the window. Then I pushed it open wide enough to peer through the blinds into darkness. I turned human again so I wouldn't get glitter over everything, and carefully climbed through.

Holding my breath, I tiptoed over bare floorboards. The space between was filled with coffins, all closed. There was no way to tell which might have vampires inside them, and that they didn't have heartbeats or seem to breathe did not help in the slightest.

The vampires wouldn't keep the recent dead in the same room they napped in, so Dr Appleton's body must be elsewhere. Sky nudged my ankle, jabbing a paw in the direction of a trapdoor in a dusty corner. I cast another unlocking spell and peered down a set of stairs into the darkness.

I could think of a million things I'd rather do than climb into the hole, but I'd heard the mortuary was in the basement along with the place they kept newer vampires until they got their blood hunger under control. If any of the corpses woke up and started walking around, the vampires were the best equipped to deal with it without terrifying the public.

The basement was dark and dusty and there was the distinct scent of something clinical almost covering up the faint smell of coppery blood. Did vampires harvest blood from the dead? Maybe I didn't want to know. I inched forwards into the dark, shuddering at the sight of several tables with bodies on them, covered with sheets. Human or vampire, I couldn't say.

Sky's faint meowing drew my attention to a coffin lying between two tables. I trod over to the smooth wooden box, and Sky reached and prodded a paper note pinned underneath the coffin. Dr Appleton's name was printed on it.

Hoping there wasn't a snoozing vampire inside, I cast a levitating spell on the coffin lid rather than touching it. My heart jump-started violently when it moved with a surprisingly loud noise, but there wasn't a vampire inside.

There was a wax dummy.

I stared, stupefied. "Is that a joke?"

"Miaow." Sky poked the note saying Dr Appleton's name again.

"He's... he's not dead. Someone swapped out the body." Did it mean he'd been revived as a vampire? Surely the vampires would have reported his revival to his loved ones at the very least so they wouldn't be surprised if he decided to pay them a visit. But I'd thought Madame Grey had examined the body herself. *What in the world is going on?*

A door swung open at the opposite end of the basement, one I hadn't noticed when I'd come in. I jumped, and the coffin lid tilted in the air. If I let go of the spell to cast a glamour on myself, I'd drop it. *Oh, no.*

Before I could move, a man strode into the room and pointed his wand at the dummy. A man who looked *very* familiar. His wand glowed, and so did the dummy. And before my eyes, it transformed until it looked like a mirror image of the man who'd just entered. Same greying hair. Same rumpled professor-style clothes.

"Knew I'd need to redo that," Dr Appleton muttered, and turned his wand on me.

"Don't hurt me," I said, backing up. "I won't tell anyone. But—why did you fake your death and let Veronica take the fall?"

He waved his wand and the coffin lid moved back into place. "I never meant to. You'll have to trust me."

I glanced down at the closed coffin. "I was just looking at a fake copy of your dead body which could prove a woman's innocence and you're telling me not to report it?"

He lowered his wand. "Veronica's safer where she is, trust me."

Not a lie. Nothing he'd said was a lie, as inexplicable as it might be. "How can I trust you when you faked your death? Was it you who killed Simeon, too? Why were you at the jail?"

"That wasn't me," he said. "And you're in more danger than you could possibly know—"

There came an ominous creaking noise from upstairs. Uh-oh. The vampires were stirring.

Dr Appleton gave me a last look and ran for the stairs, a flickering following him. In a blink, he disappeared up the ladder and out of sight.

He just used an illusion spell. I'd bet my wand he'd used it to turn himself into one of the vampires so he wouldn't be stopped. And he'd *left* me down here. *Think, Blair.* I'd never get past the vampires without being caught.

The footsteps grew louder. Sky brushed my ankles insistently, then disappeared.

Glamour. It was my only chance.

I turned into fairy mode and raised my right hand, snapping my fingers. Nothing happened. *No. I have to.*

Feet appeared on the stairs.

Glamour. Invisible. Now.

Another snap of the fingers. My body vanished. *Yes!*

I remained still until the vampire had fully climbed down the ladder, then took flight, dodged the vampire, and flew up the ladder into the room above. Unseen, I flew above the oblivious, stirring vampires, and after waving my invisible wand at the window, I soared out and into the sky.

I kept flying, adrenaline surging in my veins, until it hit me that I'd stopped shedding glitter everywhere. Wait, it'd probably turned invisible, too. Very lucky, because I'd flown right over the vampires' heads. They'd bury me alive for covering them all in glitter.

I laughed. It sounded slightly crazed. Just when I thought my life couldn't get any more bonkers. Dr Appleton really had faked his death. Since Mr Falconer had pulled a similar trick a few months ago, the vampires had employed a new string of tests on each corpse to verify whether it was real or not. Maybe they'd missed something in Dr Appleton's case, but that corpse had looked so convincing. If not for the dummy I'd seen in its place, I'd never have believed it wasn't the real deal. But why would he need to fake his death?

Had he killed Simeon? No, he hadn't lied. Perhaps it *had* been someone else in disguise at the jail. But why would there be two of him running around?

I flew in circles, thinking hard. Now I could turn invisible properly at any time I wanted without the need for a potion, all sorts of doors would open. Like jail doors. *Hmm.*

I soared over the campus, and skidded to a halt in mid-air. Several people gathered at the town border, huddled in the shelter of the trees at the forest's edge.

Had the hunters come back?

I flew lower, unseen, then remained hovering in the air. Sleepy, Dopey and Grumpy stood on the other side of the campus fence where it bordered the outskirts of town, accompanied by Dr Summers.

I knew she was involved.

I dropped lower in order to hear them, ignoring the intermittent raindrops hitting me in mid-air.

"The prison inspection will be tomorrow?" she asked.

"Yeah, we'll come back," said Grumpy. "Boss won't be here this time. He'll send us to do the grunt work. But they'll come to the same conclusion: your security forces aren't good enough."

"There's a procedure," said Dr Summers. "I can't fathom why it's taken this long, but I suppose the town's isolated state worked in its favour. I've been concerned about the state of things for a while."

Concerned enough to bring in people who trespassed illegally and helped Mrs Dailey? If ever I'd had proof that the two were working together... maybe there was a reason her husband had faked his death. Not to mention how Nina's mother had left the Nightshade Coven and had ended up pressured by Mrs Dailey as a result. I'd been too distracted to make the connection. What had the hunters promised her in return for her help? Maybe a position on whatever new council they replaced Madame Grey's with.

"I don't get it," said Dopey. "Why the prison? I thought it was the council they wanted to take."

"The council owns the police force," said Dr Summers. "Once your boss declares it unfit, it'll be a simple matter for the hunters to transfer the prisoners over to the LFPF while they work on replacing the local forces with people of their own. It won't be hard to persuade them—that prison is a dump."

Sleepy gave an eager nod. "They never should have locked her up."

I had the distinct impression he wasn't talking about Veronica.

"We'll have to help," Grumpy said. "Once they close down the prison, they'll transfer the high-security prisoners first, right?"

"Yes," said Dr Summers. "I'm afraid I won't be able to be too involved with that part. It's important to keep up impressions."

"Not to worry. Even the boss doesn't know," said Dopey. "Dunno why he bothered to come all this way, but he's not interested in handling grunt work. He'll have one of the other branch heads do it instead."

What are they talking about? Were the hunters really thinking of shutting Steve's place down? If they moved the prisoners…

Mrs Dailey would get out. And she had enough allies outside the prison to be able to utterly disappear. Meanwhile, the hunters would stick around in town, the vampires would leave and maybe the werewolves would do the same… and she'd get what she wanted after all.

No. This isn't over. If Mrs Dailey planned to make a break for it, then there'd be multiple people involved. The three idiots standing below me were a start, but they weren't actually on the wrong side of the town's border and Inquisitor Hare himself had already pardoned them for their former 'accidental' border crossing. There was no way to prove what I'd heard, and by the time I found someone to send them packing, they'd be long gone.

The inspection was tomorrow. Either I acted before then or did nothing. No other way around it.

Dr Appleton's antics had lit a spark in my brain. He'd faked his death, another person was running around using an illusion spell, and the police were utterly oblivious to magic. Sure, that made it easy for the hunters to point out their flaws, but it also gave plenty of openings to trick them into solving their own crime.

I flew back to earth and called Bethan, asking her to contact Lizzie, too. It was time for Dritch & Co to help our boss get out of jail.

The three of us met in the coffee shop where Lizzie's sister worked, Charms & Caffeine. It was packed at this time, so there was less chance of being overheard.

Once we'd all ordered lattes, I explained my unexpected run-in with Dr Appleton. I'd also texted Alissa, who was at work, explaining the same, in case she was able to help too.

"He's *alive?*" Lizzie stared at me. "Was it really him?"

"Yep." I sipped my drink. "He implied he and Veronica were working together. Turned a dummy into an exact copy of his own corpse right in front of me."

Bethan's hands clenched on her coffee cup. "My mum sure didn't tell *me* that."

"I don't understand either, but he distinctly implied he and Veronica had a plan," I said. "It's bizarre, but that's what he said. Anyway, that's not all I came here to tell you. I overheard his wife talking to the hunters. They'll be coming back tomorrow to inspect the prison, and they'll be out to make sure the police fail."

"What?" said Bethan, so loudly that a couple of people glanced in our direction. "Seriously?"

I waited to make sure nobody was listening in, and said in a low voice, "The hunters' plan is to move the prisoners to one of their own facilities afterwards. The problem is, there are certain people in that prison who are known to have worked with, or bribed, certain hunters."

"Mrs Dailey," said Bethan, her expression shadowing.

I nodded. "Yep. Blythe's mother is going to take advantage of the move to break out and probably make it look like an accident. We're going to stop her."

"Uh…" Lizzie paused. "I'm not saying it isn't serious, but I really don't get what *we* can do."

"That's why I wanted to ask if you two had any ideas," I said. "Dr Summers implied she wouldn't be involved in helping Mrs Dailey escape in person. The three hunters will be there, but they're not the brightest. I get the feeling she has other people on the outside helping out, too. Her personal assassin, for instance." Assuming it wasn't Dr Appleton.

Bethan tugged at her hair. "How'd my mother even get caught up in this?"

"Do you think she might have got locked up on purpose?" I asked Bethan. "Dr Appleton implied they had an arrangement of sorts. But it doesn't seem linked to Mrs Dailey, that I can see anyway."

"Even if she did plan it, why?" said Bethan. "She can't do anything from jail. And they took her wand. She couldn't possibly have known the hunters planned to inspect the place, could she?"

"Maybe she did," I said, some of the pieces clicking into place. "Not sure why she got herself locked up *with* Mrs Dailey, though. And I don't know who killed Simeon, either. It couldn't have been Veronica."

"To be honest, I'm lost," said Lizzie, and Bethan nodded in agreement.

I looked at the table. "I know. Believe me, I don't want any of you guys to end up in trouble either. But I don't see a way out of this which doesn't involve Mrs Dailey getting free. I just wish I could think of who else might be helping her."

"Someone in the police force?" Bethan suggested. "It's got to be someone with access to the jail, or who's really good at sneaking around."

"If they're talking to Mrs Dailey inside the jail, maybe I can sneak in and catch them at it this time," I said.

"Uh, Blair, you don't want to get arrested," Lizzie said. "And if we show up at the inspection tomorrow, they'll kick us out."

"I can turn invisible," I admitted. "Fairy magic. You guys don't have to risk it, though. Unless you can pull off an invisibility potion. Alissa's become pretty expert at it."

"The more of us are there, the more likely we'll get caught," said Lizzie. "Right? Surely there's a way to find her allies without putting our own freedom at risk."

"I don't think it'd do any harm if I showed up at the police station tomorrow," Bethan said. "I've been there at least six times this week already. That reminds me… Veronica's appeal is tomorrow. Will that go ahead with the inspection on?"

"Haven't a clue." Worry squirmed inside me. "I'm not sure even Nathan knows it's happening."

I hadn't heard from him since he'd said he'd be having a word with Steve yesterday, but if Nathan was present during the inspection, there'd be at least one person there I could trust to do the right thing.

"Uh, Blair, I don't know about this," said Lizzie. "The hunters are scary competent. If they catch us spying on them, we'll be the ones locked up. Definitely if we try to stop them moving the prisoners."

"I hope it won't come to that," I said. "I just wish I knew what Veronica and Dr Appleton were playing at. It might be she has a plan of her own, but that's probably wishful thinking."

Had they really worked together? More to the point, who was the assassin who'd killed Simeon Clarke? He'd seemed oddly familiar to me, even through the illusion. And it hadn't been Dr Appleton.

"No kidding." Bethan drummed her fingers on the table. "You know what's really unfair? They arrested Veronica on a whim, but nobody at all has been arrested for murdering Simeon."

"Er, it's hard to arrest someone who's already in jail," Lizzie said.

My insides went cold. "Yeah, about that... do you know what they did with Simeon's body? I mean, is there a funeral or anything?"

"I'm not the one you should be asking," Bethan said. "Maybe Nathan knows? Why?"

I shook my head. I'd seen one fake body today. Dr Appleton had used a spell I'd never heard of, one that had fooled even the vampires into thinking the dummy was his genuine corpse.

What if it wasn't the only time he'd done it?

Vera's lecture on metamorphosis had mostly gone over my head, but it involved transforming something into something else. I wasn't nearly at an advanced enough level of witchcraft to know the limits on that type of magic, but I was pretty sure a fake corpse that fooled the police's forensics team, Madame Grey, and a whole mortuary of vampires did not classify as conventional magic. Or common knowledge, come to that. And his assistant had said that important pieces of his research had gone missing after his death.

"What is it, Blair?" asked Lizzie.

I shook my head. "I'll check with Nathan if he's around tomorrow. Then I'll call you."

Call it a hunch, but maybe Dr Appleton had hidden his research for good reason. The only way to know for sure was to talk to the man himself, and who knew where he was hiding?

Had he helped Simeon fake his death, too? Or had someone else used his research? Either way, if Dr Appleton's fake body had fooled the vampires, it'd definitely fool the police.

We're in more trouble than I thought.

14

Firstly, I called Nathan, but heard only a dial tone. Either he was training the new security guards or talking to Steve, but either way, he was probably at the police station. I didn't like the idea of barging in there after Steve had told me in no uncertain terms to stay away, but maybe they'd be able to tell me if Simeon's body was still there or if it'd already been moved to the vampires' place.

If I told them I suspected Simeon might still be alive as well as Dr Appleton, I'd lose the little credibility I had left. Maybe the fake Dr Appleton hadn't been an assassin after all. He'd been helping Simeon escape. And now there was potentially a dangerous wizard with the ability to hypnotise people on the loose and nobody except me knew it was even possible. Simeon could use his hypnosis power on half the gargoyles if he wanted to, and nobody would be any the wiser.

Someone in there had majorly messed up, and if I

didn't at least try to warn the police before the inspection, who knew what Simeon might do?

I ran to the jail, and collided with Steve so abruptly that I went flying. Literally. Somehow, it had totally slipped my mind that I had my wings out the whole time I'd been in the café. At least I'd remembered to turn visible again.

"Ah!" I said, catching my balance. "Sorry. Hi. I actually wanted to talk to you—"

Steve glared at me. "And I wanted to talk to *you* about your harassing Dr Appleton's colleagues at the university."

My mouth dropped open. Had Dr Summers told on me to the police? Maybe she'd seen me flitting around after all. Or someone had told her I'd been asking after her. I never should have gone back.

"I wasn't harassing anyone," I said. "I was using the library."

"A likely story. The investigation is mine."

"Why aren't you investigating it, then?" I said before I could stop myself. "Did you know the hunters are coming to inspect you tomorrow? And they're looking for every excuse to fail you."

"Thank you for informing me of that, Blair," he said, in tones that suggested I was as welcome as toe fungus. "Your friend told me much the same thing. I'm considering dropping him from the security team altogether."

Oh, no. Nathan must have given him a talking-to, and he was at the risk of losing his job for it.

"You can't fire him," I protested. "He's the person training your security guards, on Madame Grey's orders. I'm guessing you just spoke to him? Is he here?"

"Go away," he snarled. "Blair Wilkes, you have done more than enough to interfere—"

"Simeon Clarke isn't dead," I burst out.

He scowled at me, startled into silence. "What are you trying to pull this time?"

"Nothing," I said. "Check Simeon Clarke's body. It's a fake, created by magic. Someone broke him out of jail and left a fake body in his place."

"Is that really the best you could do, Blair Wilkes?"

"I have nothing to gain from lying to you," I said. "You know the hunters want you deposed and the town under their own control. Mrs Dailey wants this. Have you let her speak to anyone since she was locked up?"

He took a heavy step towards me, his huge leathery wings spread wide. "No. She's kept in a place where she can't speak to anyone, without a wand. Which is where you'll be unless you give me a *very* good reason why you're wasting my time with absurd lies."

"I'm trying to help." And not doing a spectacular job of it. But even if Mrs Dailey was unable to access the outside world, Simeon was dangerous enough on his own. He'd already forced another wizard to commit murder on his behalf, not to mention nearly got several other people locked up in jail for his crime. But the body doubles were so convincing. If not for what I'd seen in the coffin, I wouldn't have known.

"I won't listen to any more of this, Blair Wilkes," he said. "Your lies have no evidence. For all I know, you're out to cause us to fail the inspection yourself."

"I don't want the town to be taken over by hunters," I said. "Listen to Nathan if you won't listen to me. Can you at least tell me where Simeon's body is?"

"He was transported to the hospital, and with any luck, he'll be six feet under by next week. Now, leave."

Shaken, I turned my back on the jail and flew off, until Steve vanished from sight.

Where now? If Nathan had had no luck talking to the police, then it was pointless trying to argue. My gaze landed on the hospital. Maybe someone there would know who'd examined Simeon's body and would be able to convince them to take another look.

I sent Alissa a text and hurried along to the hospital. Summer was typically their busiest season, since the number of broomstick-related accidents soared, but there weren't too many people in the waiting room when I entered. Just a satyr with his hoof stuck in a door, and a morose-looking witch with pimples covering every inch of visible skin. The walls were patterned with flowers, a calming contrast to my whirling thoughts. My encounter with Steve had been almost as disturbing as my experience in the vampires' basement. Fake bodies. Surely the hospital dealt with weird stuff like that occasionally, right? Look at what Mr Falconer had done. Admittedly, his own spell hadn't been anywhere near as sophisticated and the police still hadn't figured out he'd faked his death, so maybe we were doomed to failure either way.

"Blair?" Alissa walked out of one of the doors in the waiting room, holding a clipboard. "You don't need to see a healer, right?"

"No, but if you're free, I need to talk to you for a moment."

"One moment only," she said, beckoning me into the corridor.

"I was told Simeon Clarke's body was moved here

after the police looked at it." I dropped my voice. "I think they might want to take another look."

Her eyes widened. "No, it's not here. They took it to the mortuary."

"Oh." So much for that idea. "Uh... you all trained at the university, right?"

"Yes," she said warily. "But we didn't learn to transfigure dummies into fake human corpses."

"No, I figured as much." I hoped the other patients couldn't hear me. Awkward. "Is there anyone here who studied in the research division and might have known Dr Appleton?"

"Maybe Lou," said Alissa. "I probably wouldn't tell her what he did, though. Even here, it's a bit much."

You're telling me. Steve already suspected me of foul play. Yet... Simeon was a cold-blooded killer. He could force another person to commit a crime and erase their memories so they'd never recall doing it. Right now, he was even more dangerous than Mrs Dailey.

Alissa darted into a side room and returned a couple of minutes later with another nurse in tow. Lou was one of the other junior healers, a friendly-faced Asian witch.

"Oh, hey, Blair," she said. "I take it you recovered from the other night?"

"Ah... yeah, I have." Oops. I'd forgotten she'd witnessed our drunken escapades. "Uh, this is a really weird question, but I wanted to know if it's possible to use magic to create an exact replica of the human body?"

She blinked. "Possible? Not an exact copy, no. There's too much detail involved. It's one of the things we look into for training our staff... the replicas are supplied by the university, but they're not *exact.*"

"Oh," I said, jumping on the subject. "Did you ever see Dr Appleton?"

"Funny you should say that," she said. "He kept asking for corpses to practise his experiments on. Frequently. It puzzled the junior staff. Quite bizarre."

"Yeah, it sounds like he was." If the professionals here thought it couldn't be done, it meant his research really was unique. "I heard some of his research disappeared after he died. His assistant was looking for it. Do you know where it might have disappeared to?"

"I'm afraid I couldn't say," she said. "Sorry. He hasn't been here at the hospital in years."

"Never mind. Thanks." I returned to the waiting room, defeated. Simeon's body was with the vampires, who'd be wide awake by now, and Dr Appleton had taken off who knew where.

"I can try to convince them to look at the body again," Alissa said in a low voice. "But honestly, the last thing we need is the hunters deciding *we* need an inspection, too. Look what happened the last time the police barged into the hospital trying to ruin things."

I winced. "I know. It's not like I have access to the research... he must have hidden it. Even his wife didn't know. If Dr Appleton had a secret cubbyhole, it might be anywhere."

Wait a second. He'd been at Veronica's office for a reason. And... and the police had removed everything she had.

What if he'd been afraid someone would get hold of his research, and had left it with his former colleague for safekeeping?

"Alissa, I think I know what he did," I whispered. "He

left the research with Veronica—but the police confiscated everything she had."

And they might have been under Simeon's control at the time.

Oh. Oh, no.

"Seriously? Are you sure?"

"He and Veronica worked together once before," I said. "Maybe they did the same this time."

"Was their plan to get her jailed and him to end up on the run and presumed dead?" Her brows rose. "Yeah, not so sure that adds up."

"I'm still missing a few pieces,' I said. "But maybe the man himself didn't create the fake Simeon. If the research fell into the wrong hands…"

Maybe Dr Summers—no, she'd already said she hadn't found the research. But that was before Simeon's 'death'.

"I really think the only way to prove anything would be to find the real Dr Appleton," said Alissa.

"Last I saw, he was sneaking in and out of the vampires' place in order to redo the spell on his fake corpse," I said. "Maybe he's still there."

"I have an hour until my shift ends," Alissa said. "We can go back together if you like?"

I shook my head. "He'll be long gone by now. And once his funeral's over, he won't need to go back."

Should I risk invisibly breaking into the police's headquarters to see if Dr Appleton's research was there? They hadn't paid any attention to what they'd taken from Veronica's office, so chances were, they wouldn't notice if someone else had taken it. The other option was to find the real Simeon. He needed eye contact to use his powers, so if he intended to interfere in tomorrow's inspection, he couldn't have gone far. And then there was the fake Dr Appleton, the one who'd broken into the jail. Since the inspection was tomorrow, maybe he'd go back to talk to Mrs Dailey tonight. She had no other way to communicate with anyone outside. I was pretty sure I'd know if she had her own personal fairy cat or pixie.

But I do.

———

"Sky," I said, opening the flat door. "Hey, Sky."

He appeared in a flash of fur. "Miaow."

"I need your help." I let the door close behind me. "I think Simeon Clarke is alive and planning to help Mrs Dailey break out of jail. Would you be able to find him if he's in town?"

"Miaow." He bowed his head, looking dejected.

"I guess not." I scratched behind his ears. "I think he or one of her other helpers might be at the jail tonight. It'll be our last chance to catch them sneaking in to talk to her before tomorrow's inspection."

Sure, breaking into the jail again was a bad idea, but I didn't need to break in to catch Mrs Dailey's people. Invisible, there was little I couldn't do.

Sky rolled onto his back, demanding to be stroked. I obligingly crouched down. "Please," I said. "Don't worry, I won't turn you invisible this time, but I'd really appreciate it if you came with me for moral support."

"Miaow." Sky looked unimpressed.

I sighed. "I'll buy ten stacks of bubble wrap for you to ruin."

Sky stretched out and purred. Now we were getting somewhere.

———

For the second time that week, I made my way to the jail under cover of darkness.

I left Alissa a bunch of instructions to pass onto Bethan and Lizzie if this went badly—chiefly, finding the real Dr Appleton, stopping Simeon from hypnotising anyone else, and finding the identity of the fake professor. I had to admit that I'd rather deal with Simeon myself, if just because I was immune to his powers. Not to mention he was a dangerous killer, and the last thing I wanted was for him to hurt any of my friends.

I flew as fast as I possibly could, Sky running beside me. He didn't need to turn invisible to disappear into the night. If not for his one white paw, I'd never have been able to see him in the darkness. More gargoyles prowled around the streets than usual. I slowed down as we neared the jail, glad the glitter was invisible. Sky, meanwhile, vanished into the shadows.

Hope he knows what he's doing.

Gargoyles blocked the entire road leading to the jail, alert for any signs of trouble. Maybe Mrs Dailey wouldn't be able to consult her people tonight after all.

A huge gargoyle lumbered out of the jail and began to walk away, forcing me to step aside to avoid being knocked out by one of his wings. His steps were oddly tottering, like he was drunk, but none of the others gave him a second glance. I frowned. Gargoyles drunk on duty? Was he under mind control?

I moved to follow him, but two more gargoyles appeared behind me, forcing me to duck into an alley to avoid them. By the time they'd gone, so was the possibly-drunk guard. I stared around the darkened street in confusion. Had he vanished into thin air? There weren't many people around at all. Maybe the presence of all the security had frightened people into staying in tonight. All I could see was a lone drunk staggering towards the high street.

Hang on a moment. I knew that guy.

Leopold.

I picked up the pace, following him. His drunken steps were so familiar. In fact, he walked just like that gargoyle I'd just seen.

Leopold broke into a run, like he sensed my presence. I beat my wings and flew behind him, grabbing the scruff of his neck. He yelped, and I quickly covered his mouth with my hand.

"It was *you*," I hissed. "You're working for Mrs Dailey, aren't you?"

Why hadn't I guessed? I'd seen him running around at night enough times that I should have recognised his drunken stumble when he'd been pretending to be Dr Appleton in the bushes outside the jail.

"I don't know what you're talking about!" he yelped. "Let me go."

"You know I can tell you're lying," I said. "You were talking to her just then, weren't you? I'd rather nobody else died. Faked or not."

He winced. "I had to."

"It was you I ran into the other night, too, wasn't it? Disguised as Dr Appleton. What did she do to you?"

"I thought I was applying for a job," he mumbled. "At the university."

"*Oh.* Dr Summers?"

He nodded frantically. "I was supposed to interview as Dr Appleton's assistant, but she showed up instead. She said that Dr Appleton was being investigated for fraud and had some important research hidden. I was meant to find it, but then—then she told me he'd likely faked his death, using the research. She ordered me to find it but not to give it directly to her, because she was being investigated, too. So I…"

"So you stole the research," I said. "And—*you* faked Simeon's body?"

"The spell wasn't that hard to copy," he mumbled. "It was designed that way, but she said Dr Appleton regretted it and wanted to destroy the research before it got out."

Whoa. I'd been right after all. "Why did you go ahead with it?" I asked. "You must have known it was illegal."

His face crumpled. "She blackmailed me. I just wanted out."

"If you do as Mrs Dailey says and help her escape tomorrow, the whole town will be taken over by hunters," I said. "You know that, right? And two criminals will walk free. Do the right thing."

"I—" he cut himself off. "You're right. I have to go to the police."

"Go there now. Trust me, it's for the best."

He nodded, biting his lip, and took a step forwards.

There was a bright flash. I threw up my hands instinctively to block the glare of light, and when I removed them, Leopold lay unmoving in front of me.

"No!"

Another blast of light caused me to stumble back. A familiar pressure burst behind my eyes, and then there was darkness.

———

I blinked awake. Someone was standing over me. Two someones with huge wingspans… gargoyles. I jumped to my feet, my fairy wings beating.

"Blair Wilkes." Ink Face loomed above me. "Did you kill this man?"

My heart climbed into my throat. Leopold lay at my feet. "No. Someone hit him with a spell from behind." *Simeon. It must have been Simeon.* I peered into the dark, but of course, the killer was long gone.

"I didn't kill him," I whispered. "I didn't even have my wand out."

Steve's voice said from behind me, "Who knows what tricks you can do in that fairy disguise of yours?"

I spun to face him. "It's the truth," I said. If I was about to get arrested, I might as well lay all the cards out. "Leopold confessed to me that it was him who faked Simeon's death and broke him out of jail. The real Simeon —just killed him." I'd felt him try to use his psychic powers on me. I'd never forget that feeling in a hurry. I was lucky I had a memory left.

Steve glanced down at Leopold's crumpled body. "Your ridiculous explanation can only be backed up by the man himself—who's dead. Convenient."

"I know what it looks like. But believe me—I didn't kill him. My wand's in my pocket, you can check." My hands were shaking. So was my whole body. Simeon had been hiding close by after all. He might even have used his power on Steve.

Two gargoyles closed in on me. One pulled out handcuffs.

"Please," I said. "Please believe me. If you fail the inspection tomorrow, Mrs Dailey's plotting to escape."

And she didn't need Leopold any more. That's why she'd killed him.

"If the inspection fails, you'll be off somewhere much worse than our jail, Blair Wilkes," Steve said.

My heart sank like a stone. He knew he was going to fail. He just wanted to take me down with him, then I'd be out of his wings forever.

15

I hadn't exactly planned my grand confrontation to take place from *inside* the jail, without a wand. The police had taken it off me after my arrest, and I was to stay in a cell until my trial. Considering the inspection was first thing tomorrow, I had my doubts I'd get the chance to explain myself anytime soon. Meanwhile, Simeon walked free. With Leopold dead, Mrs Dailey had covered her tracks well. I wasn't even in the right part of the jail to speak to her. I hadn't yet been upgraded to one of the nice posh cells for long-term inmates, but was instead stuck in the foul-smelling dismal area used to detain people overnight.

If you ask me, they'll fail the inspection for the state of this place alone. Unless the other paranormal prisons were worse. The LFPF... was that my fate? If the inspection failed, all the prisoners would be moved somewhere more secure. Including me.

I couldn't have picked a worse time to get arrested. Sure, I might be able to turn invisible, but it would be more useful if I could walk through walls like Sky. They'd even taken my levitating boots, leaving me in a pair of flimsy shoes that belonged to someone whose feet were much larger than mine. I shuffled over to the door and pressed my hands to the cold bars. I didn't have a were-wolf or vampire's super strength, so there was no chance of breaking out. Besides, if I broke out, I'd either get caught or end up doomed to a life on the run.

No. it can't end like this.

Some indeterminate amount of time later, there came the sound of voices. A number of people had come into the jail, from the noise level.

"As you can see, the place has been in need of refurbishing for years," said Steve. "These are the holding cells where we keep prisoners overnight as a deterrent. It's an effective one."

The inspection's on. The voices grew louder, and then several people passed by my cell. One of the gargoyles—Ink Face—scowled through the bars of my cell as though to check I was still there. I gave him an innocent smile. *Not doing anything, honest.*

Shockingly, all I heard from the hunters were mutters about how filthy the place was.

"Did I hear you're training a new security team?" one of them asked.

"Yes," said Clare, the gargoyle who usually staffed the front desk. "You might not have heard, but we had plans to replace the whole team before the hunters ever came here."

The grumpy gargoyle receptionist climbed a hundred points in my estimation. I hadn't known she'd be accompanying the inspection. Their patrol halted, and Ink Face gave me another glower as he walked past my cell again. As he did so, there was an odd flicker, but it disappeared as soon as he was gone.

"Yes, we did," Nathan put in. "I'm training the team myself. Now, if it turns out we need backup, the plan was always to reach out to you, but it's not necessary to replace any of our people. As for the facility, Madame Grey has made a generous offer to fund the construction of a facility to rival one of your own."

My mouth fell open. *Thanks, Madame Grey.* That was crafty of her. The hunters wouldn't need to move all the prisoners if a new jail was under construction here. Not that it got Steve off the hook. Oddly, Sleepy, Dopey and Grumpy weren't anywhere within sight either. I'd been sure they'd said they were accompanying the inspection. Had Madame Grey caught them first?

"We will evaluate the results," said the hunter. "In the meantime, I'm told there's a trial this morning."

"Yes… there is," said Steve, sounding flustered. "I was under the impression this would take much longer."

I sat back in my cell, thoroughly puzzled. It didn't sound like the gargoyles were anywhere near as unprepared as I'd feared. Not to mention the hunters working for Mrs Dailey were nowhere in sight. Had her plan failed, or was this part of it?

A few minutes later, Clare the gargoyle receptionist walked up to my cell and unlocked the door.

"Uh… good morning?" I said.

"You've been granted an early trial, before Veronica Eldritch's," she said. "Consider yourself lucky."

They were putting me on trial now? Had Madame

Grey pulled some strings? Someone had been busy, that was for certain.

Once I was in handcuffs again, the gargoyles shepherded me into the same trial room as before. Like during Veronica's trial, it was packed out with gargoyles, and Madame Grey sat in the same seat she had last time.

No wonder Simeon and the others hadn't made trouble. She must have decided to attend the inspection in person.

Our gazes met, and she gave me a nod of reassurance. A moment later, Nina and Alissa entered the room. Alissa glanced my way, and I tried to catch her eye. *Did you tell everything to Madame Grey?* She must have. But that didn't explain the absence of a certain group of hunters. Not to mention Mrs Dailey remained incarcerated and who even knew where Simeon and Dr Appleton were. Or his wife, come to that. I hadn't the faintest idea what Nina was doing here, either. But even Madame Grey wouldn't be able to perform a miracle with no evidence. And Nathan had disappeared. Maybe Steve had ordered him not to attend the trial.

"Sit down," Steve snapped at me, lumbering in with his wings out and his least professional glower. *Why?* It didn't sound like the inspection was going anywhere nearly as badly as I'd feared. Not that there was a high bar as far as Steve was concerned.

I sat in the central chair, and cringed as the chains on the seat sprang to life, wrapping around my body. I looked like a mechanical mummy. At least I'd put my wings away, otherwise it'd have been even more uncomfortable.

"Let's get this over with," Steve said, seating himself.

"Blair, do you deny that you were found beside the dead body of a man yesterday?"

"No, but he wasn't dead when I started talking to him." Ack. I should probably have worded that better. "I mean, someone hit him with a spell and knocked me out. I didn't kill him."

"We looked at the body," added Alissa. "From his injuries, he was definitely hit by a spell from behind. Not only was Blair in front of him at the time, she didn't even have her wand out, and she was unconscious when the police found her."

Steve's eyes narrowed. And I saw a familiar flash within them.

Mind control.

Oh *no*. Simeon had got to him. But when?

"That's not good enough," Steve said. "There's been no sign of this mysterious killer, but a lot of reports of Blair being in places she wasn't supposed to be in."

"Curiosity doesn't make one a killer," said Madame Grey. "It's only natural that Blair would want her boss to be freed from custody if she believed her to be innocent. As do I."

"It sounds like she's been harassing staff at the university," Steve said, "and is believed to have broken into this very facility at least once. Some paperwork went missing."

"That was Dr Appleton's research," I said. "If you find him, you'll see that he was looking into metamorphosis, and if you examine his body or Simeon's, you'll see that they were very convincing fakes created by the same spell. Leopold was in the middle of confessing to me that he was coerced into creating the double of Simeon's body under duress when he was killed."

"A likely story," he said. "And where is the real Dr Appleton hiding?"

"You tell me," I said. "I saw and spoke to him."

"You're not helping your case, Miss Wilkes," he said. "The man was found dead in the office you work in. Maybe you killed him and not Ms Eldritch."

"Neither of us killed him, because he's not dead," I said.

"Enough!" Steve shouted. His eyes were scarily blank.

Simeon's close by. He must be. After all, he required eye contact to use mind control.

Wait. Might he be in this room?

I let my gaze travel across the gargoyles standing beside the door, and spotted a flickering in the corner of my eye.

I cleared my throat. "Look at that." I pointed at Ink Face. "He's flickering."

"What?" Ink Face snapped. "Be quiet. You're not supposed to be talking to me."

"You're not supposed to be here." He'd been standing at the very back as though to avoid attention. Clever.

"Flickering," said Madame Grey. "If I may."

She waved her wand. Ink Face raised a hand, and abruptly, he flew back, slamming into the wall.

And turned back into Simeon.

With a snarl, he spun around, only to find himself surrounded by gargoyles.

"Blindfold him," I shouted. "Before he uses that mind-control power again. He's been using it through this whole trial."

"Impossible," said Steve. "That man is dead!"

"Clearly, he isn't." Madame Grey waved her wand, and

a strip of material appeared, wrapping around Simeon's eyes. "Simeon, do tell us. How did you fake your death?"

He squirmed as two gargoyles grabbed him, fury twisting his features. But he wasn't escaping anytime soon. "I used a body double," he ground out. "Created with magic."

Steve looked utterly stupefied. "How is this possible?"

"Simeon faked his death and Leopold helped him escape," I said quickly. "Leopold had just confessed to me when he died. He was going to come and tell the police. I'm guessing Simeon's the one who killed him."

"How was the body replaced?" Alissa put in, her eyes on the door as though expecting something to happen. "How did it look so convincing?"

"It was a metamorphosed body created using experimental magic," Simeon said. "It's fool-proof. And you'll never get that research back."

"Whose research?" asked Madame Grey.

"Mine," said Dr Appleton, striding into the room.

16

All eyes turned to face the newcomer. Simeon's mouth fell open and he sagged in the gargoyle's grip. Not part of his plan, then. Or mine, come to that. The real Dr Appleton had decided to show up after all.

"It was my research," he said. "Nobody knew I'd used it to fake my own death."

From the look on Simeon's face, he hadn't either. Only Madame Grey looked unsurprised at the professor's sudden appearance. And Alissa, though she'd turned to whisper something to Nina. *Did she plan this?*

"You're dead," Steve said, staring at the professor as though expecting him to transform into a teacup before his eyes.

Dr Appleton moved further into the room, so everyone could see him. "No. I used the spell to create a replica of my own body before my 'death'."

"Why exactly did you do that?" asked Madame Grey.

"An innocent woman is in jail because she's believed to have killed you."

"It was the only way," he said. "I was at Veronica's office initially because my ex-wife was after the research and I knew she wanted to use it for herself. I thought Veronica would be able to disguise it among her own paperwork. Unfortunately, it slipped my mind that she was absent from the town and would likely think I was an intruder when she came back. We confronted one another, and I left. When I did, I ran into my wife, who had guessed I planned to hide the evidence. I had no choice but to retreat to my hideout, where I'd prepared the body to fake my death when the time came."

"You're saying Dr Summers was responsible for you faking your death?" Steve looked like he wished *he'd* been the one to fake his death and disappear so he wouldn't have to deal with this insanity. Too bad for him.

"Yes," Dr Appleton said. "I heard her speaking to the hunters on the phone on campus, and from what I heard, it sounded like they promised her a place on their council if they took power."

Steve turned to the handful of hunters still gathered at the edge of the room. "Is that true?"

They all looked baffled. "We received no such phone call," said one of them. "Our supervisor told us that we were to apply to a company called Eldritch & Co to work for their security forces."

"That was the cover story," said Dr Appleton. "My ex-wife initially called their main office under an alias and then passed on their information to Veronica Eldritch in the hope that one of her employees would call them to interview for the town's security team."

"So it was her?" I fidgeted, wishing someone would take the chains off the seat. My back was really starting to ache. "Veronica was set up," I added to Steve and the others in explanation. "It was supposed to look like Dritch & Co had *chosen* to invite the hunters here, but the file was planted among the genuine ones by someone else."

Dr Appleton nodded. "Yes. Veronica and I used to be business partners, which is why I chose to leave my paperwork with her. In our initial discussion, I told her the nature of my research and why I had to fake my death."

"So she knew you planned to frame her?" I never quite understood Veronica's decisions at the best of times, but this had me stumped.

"She knew," he said. "The hunters planned to take your company out of the picture and replace the curse on its owner with something more permanent."

The hunters looked outraged. "We certainly did not plan to harm anyone in this town," said one of them, a large blond man.

The door opened, and another gargoyle appeared. "There's been an incident," he growled. "We found three people tied up in the bushes behind the back fence of the university campus. Hunters, apparently."

"What?" yelped Steve.

"Bring them in," Madame Grey said. If I didn't know better, I'd say she looked almost amused.

Sleepy, Dopey and Grumpy sidled into the room, to further confusion.

"Tied up in the bushes?" Madame Grey said. "Now, how might that have occurred?"

"They're part of our team," said the blond hunter. "Or… they were. They never showed up at the meeting point today."

"Looks like they're about to see what the inside of a cell looks like," I said, grinning despite myself. Alissa caught my eye and winked. I should have known she'd come through for me. "Steve, these three hunters are the ones who conspired with Dr Summers. I'm guessing they were on their way to see her when someone ambushed them."

"They were let off with a minor caution for trespassing once before," Nathan said, walking in through the half-open door. "I was surprised they'd be chosen for this mission, considering."

The small group of remaining hunters all looked abashed. "How did this happen?" said the blond one.

"Him." I pointed at Simeon, who remained chained between two gargoyles on the other side of the door. "He's been using mind control on anyone who gets too close since you showed up. And he's been working on the police for much longer. He stole Dr Appleton's research from your office. Or he had Leopold do it."

"How did his research end up in our office?" Steve demanded.

"He told you, he hid it with Veronica's other notes, which you confiscated," I said. "Right, Dr Appleton?"

He nodded frantically. "Yes. I hid the research, but once it fell into the police's hands, the wizard who died yesterday stole it and used my metamorphosing spell to help Simeon escape from jail. There was nothing I could do. If I'd known the conspirators had someone capable of using mind control on their side, I might have been able to stop them, but even Veronica didn't expect it."

"I see," said Madame Grey. "I'll send someone to find Dr Summers immediately and bring her in. I'd suggest you question Veronica to see if her story matches his, Steve."

Wait. We still haven't caught the person pulling the strings.

There was just one more criminal to unmask.

"I'm the one giving orders," Steve said ineffectually. He nodded to two of the gargoyles in the now considerably overcrowded area by the door. "Fetch her."

"Hang on," I said quickly. "Someone else worked with those three hunters and gave Simeon orders from inside the jail itself."

"Quiet," Steve snapped, but there was nowhere near as much force in his voice as usual. He was outnumbered by people who understood the situation much better than he did.

Madame Grey spoke quietly into her phone, probably ordering the other witches to find Dr Summers. Meanwhile, the hunters awkwardly shuffled aside when yet more gargoyles brought Veronica in.

"The handcuffs are unnecessary," I said, wondering when someone was going to undo the chains on my seat. "She's innocent."

"She admitted to meeting with the victim before his death!" said Steve.

"Clearly he's not a victim," said Madame Grey waspishly. "He's standing right there, plainly alive."

Steve looked like Christmas had been cancelled. "This is ridiculous. Are any of the victims actually dead?"

"Leopold is," I said. "Since I saw him drop dead in

front of me. The same can't be said for the others. But if you lock Simeon up in the same place as the person he worked with, she'll find another way to use his power to engineer an escape. If you didn't notice him use his mind-control power on you, then clearly, he should be put somewhere else. For everyone's safety."

"That's not your call to make," said Steve. "Besides, all the evidence suggests Simeon acted alone, and until he gives us the name of the person he worked with, that stands."

"Oh, that would be Mrs Dailey," said Madame Grey. "I've heard multiple reports that she's had contact with all the people involved in this scheme, including Dr Summers, the three hunters you found on campus, and of course Simeon and Leopold."

"Mrs Dailey is in jail!" Steve almost screamed. He whirled on Simeon. "Did she give you orders?"

His mouth pressed together. Then he snapped. "Yes, she did. She contacted me before she was jailed herself, because she needed the help of someone else with mind-magic. She taught me how to use mind control on the guards. I was supposed to help her escape when the hunters were transporting her to their own facility."

"I think that clears things up," said Madame Grey. "In the meantime..." She turned to the hunters. "As you can see, some of your people are involved in illicit activities. You might want to look into that before attempting to displace us. Perhaps more thorough vetting of your employees would be in order... if that's the case, you're more than welcome to ask Veronica Eldritch for direction."

"I agree," Nathan said. "We have a sufficient enough

team of our own, and more than enough citizens willing to do the right thing."

"Exactly," I said. "I think they might want to look at their own people first, before judging ours."

"To what end was all this meant to accomplish?" Steve demanded, looking from Simeon to the hunters as though begging for an explanation he could grasp. "Mrs Dailey? She can't communicate with anyone."

"I think it's clear that she can," said Madame Grey. "And as it happens, I agree that this prison has its limits, particularly for criminals with mind powers. I would support her being transported to another facility—supervised by myself of course. Would that be possible?"

The hunters started when she addressed them. "That can be arranged," said the blond man.

"I would suggest removing Mr Clarke from the facility while you question Mrs Dailey again," added Madame Grey. "It's best to assess whether or not any of the guards are affected by his abilities before we take action. Luckily, it seems that he can only affect one person at any given moment, and only for a short length of time."

Veronica cleared her throat. "And I am to walk free, since it's clear I committed no crimes?"

"Same here," I added, pointedly rattling the chains on my chair.

Steve looked about ready to explode. "Right. Lock up Mr Clarke, release Ms Eldritch and Blair—Blair Wilkes." He sounded like the words pained him to speak.

Thanks to the crowd in the doorway, it took forever to get out once the gargoyles had freed me from the chains. I managed to squeeze out of the room through a gap between two gargoyles, and found Bethan and Lizzie waiting in the lobby.

"Hey!" said Lizzie. "Glad they let you both out."

Bethan beamed at me. "It was a collective effort for Dritch & Co."

"Which part did you two do?" I asked. "Tying up the hunters in the bushes? Or finding Dr Appleton?"

"The hunters," said Lizzie. "We also spiked the guards' coffee with a sleeping draught, so new guards who weren't under Simeon's control would take over. But we didn't count on him actually going into the trial."

"It all worked out in the end, though," I said, unable to stop smiling. "How'd you know the hunters would come to campus?"

"We watched the border all night waiting for them to show up," said Bethan. "Alissa and Nina watched the jail. We were in constant contact. Also, your cat helped."

I seriously owed them all for this. "So Dr Appleton came out of hiding just in time. And Dritch & Co…"

"Will be back to normal soon," said Veronica, passing by to hug her daughter. "Thank you for the help."

"Thanks for telling me you got jailed on purpose," Bethan said.

"I was the target of an assassin," she said matter-of-factly.

"Not exactly," Bethan said. "Seriously, you'd probably have been fine. Your security spells are enough."

The police brought Dr Summers in as we were leaving the building with Alissa and Nina. Steve had kept Dr Appleton back for further questioning, and to testify against his ex-wife. I hoped she'd get a long sentence, too.

"That'd teach her for telling tales on me to Steve," I muttered to Alissa.

"Did she?" Alissa raised an eyebrow. "It's really lucky you told me all about what Simeon might try to do today. We went in with about six plans."

"I didn't expect Dr Appleton to come back," I admitted. "That made things easier. Er, Nina, why did you come?"

"Your cat fetched me," she said. "Alissa needed someone to back her up, someone who knew Dr Summers was a crook. I didn't know she'd go *that* far to gain the council's favour."

"I appreciate it," I said. "Really."

"We took shifts at the border last night," Alissa added. "We figured, like you did, that the hunters wouldn't show up all at once. The ones working with her would arrive separately for a rendezvous before their plan went ahead."

"Those three really aren't bright," I said. "I wonder which prison they'll go in."

"Their own, no doubt," said Nathan, from my other side. "They need to be trialled by their own people, too. I doubt they'll be let off with a caution this time around."

"Good," I said. "Anyway, since when did Madame Grey offer to fund the construction of a new prison?"

"Since I asked," Nathan said. "I'm in charge of the security team, and that puts me as Steve's equal."

"I'm sure he'll be thrilled about that," I said. I didn't really care what Steve thought. He was lucky to still have a job at all.

"Miaow," said Sky, wrapping himself around my legs. I scratched him behind the ears.

"Thanks," I said. "I owe you. All of you."

The hunters would be back. That much was certain. But today, victory was ours.

———

Work went back to normal immediately. First thing on Monday morning, Dritch & Co was open for business, and more popular than ever.

Admittedly, our distraction levels were high, since Veronica insisted on coming to tell us in person every time she received an update from the police. According to her, Dr Summers had received a special promise from the hunters for her coven to be allowed a position on their new council. Instead, she'd be getting a jail sentence, while Nina's new coven had invited in the other Nightshade witches who found themselves without a leader. Blythe's mother was off to the Lancashire Prison for Paranormals, supervised by Madame Grey. I doubted she'd be able to conduct any schemes from in there. As for Simeon, he'd be going back into a closed cell in one of their other jails, as far from Mrs Dailey as possible.

I definitely hadn't seen the last of Inquisitor Hare. He'd all but promised me, after all. Yet it was hard to feel threatened when the hunters had departed with their tails between their legs. I had no doubt they'd think long and hard before sending anyone else here.

When the workday ended, I found Nathan waiting for me outside the door.

"How'd it go?" he asked.

"Pretty great," I said. "Back to normal. And you?"

"I saw to it that Mrs Dailey was properly transported

to the prison," he said. "She tried sweet-talking the guards, but it didn't work."

"Good," I said. "I take it Sleepy, Dopey and Grumpy are in disgrace?"

"They're temporarily suspended. They'll have to return to the normal world for a while."

"Pity for them. Veronica said Simeon got taken to another prison, but Dr Summers is staying in this one."

"Yes, she is," he said. "Steve argued that she ought to stay here for her sentence, since she's not a murderer."

"She's almost as dangerous, considering what that research can do," I said. The research itself was back in Dr Appleton's hands, and he'd returned to his position at the university. I wasn't best pleased with him for hiding while Leopold ran amok with his research, but he *had* feared for his life.

"She won't make any more trouble," said Nathan. "As for Simeon, he'll be transported to the other jail tomorrow. The guards are still baffled on how he managed to fool them with that illusion charm. You saw through his spell, but nobody else did. Even Madame Grey."

"Uh. I thought she did."

He shook his head. "Even the mind control went unseen. I have a feeling that only you saw it, Blair."

"What? That can't be possible. I'm not—I can't be…"

"You see the truth of a person," Nathan said. "Apparently in more than one way."

"Who told you that?"

"Madame Grey herself, of course."

Just when I thought I was done with surprises. Life would calm down a little now, but I didn't think the paranormal world would ever be normal. And thank goodness for that.

When Nathan and I parted ways, I walked home to my flat in high spirits, ready for my witchcraft lesson that evening. Madame Grey would be there, and I'd tell her all about…

I stopped, my foot on the doorstep. A piece of rolled-up paper was wedged underneath the door. It unfurled when I picked it up, shedding glitter.

A note from my father: *If Inquisitor Hare has targeted you, Blair, leave Fairy Falls. Your life depends on it.*

ABOUT THE AUTHOR

Elle Adams lives in the middle of England, where she spends most of her time reading an ever-growing mountain of books, planning her next adventure, or writing. Elle's books are humorous mysteries with a paranormal twist, packed with magical mayhem.

She also writes urban and contemporary fantasy novels as Emma L. Adams.

Find Elle on Facebook at https://www.facebook.com/pg/ElleAdamsAuthor/

www.ingramcontent.com/pod-product-compliance
Lightning Source LLC
Chambersburg PA
CBHW020812190726
48285CB00006B/2256